I Didn't Plan This

Kelsey Gallant

Published by Blobfish Books

I Didn't Plan This / Kelsey Gallant
ISBN: 9781719801164
BISAC: Fiction/JUV/Social Issues/Friendship

Summary: Alanna has her future perfectly planned out, but upon starting
seventh grade, she learns that life doesn't always happen according to plan.

[1. Friendship—Fiction. 2. Best Friends—Fiction. 3. Schools—Fiction.
4. Crushes—Fiction. 5. Siblings—Fiction.]

Dedicated to all my students at Elm Street Middle School, 2015-2016 school year

Prologue

Our ages lined up perfectly. Travis was one week and two days younger than Lacey, and Daniel was one month and three weeks older than me. We were next door neighbors, but if you didn't know us, it would be hard to tell who lived in which house. A long time ago, back when Daniel and I were babies and Travis and Lacey were two years old, our neighbors knew us in pairs based on our families—Travis and Daniel were brothers, Lacey and Alanna were sisters. But it didn't take long for them to stop thinking about us in regard to our families, and start thinking about us in regard to how they saw us: Travis and Lacey, Daniel and Alanna. Always.

I remember the day we planned out our futures. Daniel and I were five, and Lacey and Travis were seven. The four of us were hanging out together that day, as we always did when we weren't broken down into our pairs. Lacey was the leader of the group.

"Guys," Lacey said, looking around at Daniel, Travis, and me all flopped out in the grass beneath our favorite oak tree. We had just spent the last half hour running around both of our yards, playing tag. "Guys, listen up."

Daniel and I had been sort of tackling each other, and Travis had been tossing a squishy rubber ball up and down. But we all stopped what we were doing and looked at Lacey.

"While we're resting from playing tag, I think we should all talk about what we want to do when we grow up." Lacey's second-grade class had recently held a Career Day, in which all the kids got to bring in a parent and the parents told the kids about their jobs. It had put Lacey on a real "When I grow up" kick.

"I wanna live in a mansion," Daniel said. "With a bowling alley inside."

"Me too," I agreed. "And it should also have a pool. Maybe me and Daniel can get married and live in the mansion together."

"Yeah!" exclaimed Daniel.

"Me and Lacey can also get married, and we'll live in a mansion next to you guys," said Travis.

2

"Yes," agreed Lacey. "Travis and I will get married first, since we're older. We'll move into a giant mansion next to a beautiful lake. Then two years later, Daniel and Alanna can have their wedding at our mansion."

"And after our wedding, we'll move into a mansion that's even gianter than yours," Daniel added. "With pools and bowling alleys and a bunch of cool stuff. But it'll be right next door to your mansion, so you guys can come visit."

"And all of our kids will be best friends with each other, just like us!" I exclaimed.

"Perfect," said Lacey.

So that was our plan. We never discussed it again after that, but it didn't matter. I knew it would happen. A long time off in the future, after we were all grown up, Lacey would marry Travis, and I would marry Daniel. I never imagined that anything would change our minds.

Until the start of junior high.

Chapter 1
The Last Day

"Man," Travis leaned back into the grass, hands behind his head, as the breeze blew gently around us. It was a hot day toward the end of August, so the breeze felt nice.

"Woman," I said, since Travis hadn't added anything else to his exclamation of "Man." I saw Daniel give me a funny look. "Man, woman, get it?" I said. "Why do people not say that, anyway? People say 'man' all the time, but nobody ever says, 'Woman!'"

Lacey yawned and rolled her eyes. "I don't know, look it up." That was Lacey's answer for everything, except for things to which she did know the answer, in which case she'd tell you the literal, exact answer.

"Nah, it's not that important." I said. "What were you saying 'man' about anyway, Travis?"

Travis, who was still in a relaxed position and now had his eyes closed, replied, "I was just going to say, 'Man, what a nice day.' You don't get days like this every day."

"True," I agreed. "You really don't."

The sun was bright and hot, but we were sheltered underneath our favorite oak tree. It had been our special hangout place for as long as I could remember. It was the very place where, seven years ago, we'd decided that Daniel and I would marry each other and Travis and Lacey would marry each other.

I looked around at my sister, my sister's best friend/future husband, and my own best friend/future husband. Life was good. Very good.

"What a perfect day to end our summer vacation," Lacey commented.

Daniel groaned. "Why'd you have to remind me?"

"Remind you of what? That school's starting tomorrow?"

"Yeah."

"Oh, come on, Daniel. You should be excited about

school starting. You're going into junior high!"

The way our district was set up, you went to lower elementary school for kindergarten through third grade, upper elementary school for fourth through sixth grade, junior high school for seventh and eighth grade, and high school for ninth through twelfth. Daniel and I were going into seventh grade. Lacey and Travis were starting high school.

Daniel rolled his eyes. "Junior high. You and Travis have told us all about it, remember? Popularity contests. Who's cooler. Mean guys in the locker room and on the bus. Snooty girls who only care about their clothes and their face."

"Well, that's only some people," said Travis, sitting up and brushing off his back. "There are nice kids in junior high as well."

"Yeah, and even if there aren't, we'll still have each other," I gave Daniel a big, beaming smile. "Best friends forever, right, Daniel?"

He nodded. "Still, though. What if I'm not cool enough? What if everyone laughs at me or something?"

"Who *cares* if everyone laughs at you?" I said.

"I do."

"Oh." I shrugged. Personally, I didn't think being

laughed at would be so horrible. As long as Daniel and I were together, who cared what the other kids thought of me?

"Junior high's not too bad," said Lacey. "It's at least better than elementary school. Tons more after-school activities you can get involved in."

Lacey was the queen of after-school activities. The year before, she'd been part of band and chorus (which usually met during school, but there were a few after-school practices), history club, debate club, student council, National Science Bowl, and Future Problem Solvers. All I'd been involved in was soccer.

"I don't really know what after-school activities *to* get involved in," said Daniel.

"We could do soccer again," I suggested.

Daniel made a face. "*You* can do soccer again. I don't really want to."

Soccer without Daniel? It was unthinkable. We'd always done everything together. Even though soccer wasn't *really* together, since I'd been in a girls' league and he'd been in a boys' league. But still, Daniel and I always did the *same* activities.

"Well..." I said, thinking about it. "We could do, I

don't know, baking club? *Is* there a baking club?"

Daniel shrugged. "I don't know, but I'm not going to worry about what activities I want to sign up for until after school starts. I want to meet people first, see what they're doing, and then see if anything strikes my interest."

"That's good thinking," Lacey encouraged him. "And don't be afraid to try a bunch of new things. That way you can find out what you really like."

All this talk about trying new things was a little bit alarming to me, since new things could be kind of scary. I liked things to stay the same. But I didn't want to worry about it, so I said, "Anyone up for a game of catch?"

Lacey, Daniel, and Travis all roused themselves and stood up. "Let's do it!" said Travis.

It was the last day before junior high. The last day before my life got turned upside-down.

Chapter 2

Madalaine

"Alanna! Have you seen my brush? I need my brush. Where is it? Oh my word, I'm going to be late, I know it. I'm going to be late for my first day of high school."

Lacey was in a frenzy, tearing around the house looking for her misplaced hairbrush. I had no idea where it was. I had just gotten up. I didn't have to be at the bus stop for another forty-five minutes, whereas Lacey's bus was leaving in just ten minutes.

"Mom! Have you seen my brush?" Lacey ran down the hall to the bathroom, where Mom was curling her hair. Both of our parents worked, but Mom only worked part-time so she could be home when we were home. Mom would have to leave for work shortly after I would have to leave for school. She'd be back by the time Lacey got home.

I ate my breakfast while Lacey dashed around, gathering up her phone, her backpack, a change of shoes, and a sweatshirt. For someone who'd spent three hours the night before making sure everything was prepared and entirely ready, she sure had a lot of extra preparation to do. At 7:03, she was out the door with two minutes to get to the bus stop. She would make it. The bus stop wasn't far away from our house. She'd probably even have time to chat with Travis before the bus arrived.

Now it was my turn to rush around like a lunatic getting ready, although I didn't have as much to do as Lacey. I didn't need to put on makeup, for example, or do my hair. Lacey didn't wear much makeup, just a little, but still, a little bit took time. Also, she always had to have her hair pulled back in a perfect ponytail, every straight blond hair perfectly in place. I didn't really bother with my hair, I just wore it down all the time and let it fall however it naturally fell.

I made it to the bus stop with several minutes to spare. A couple eighth-graders were already there, so I said hi to them and then stood waiting for Daniel. A moment later, he arrived.

"Hey," he said to me.

"Hey back," I said. I could tell he'd dressed very carefully for the first day of school. His shirt was one I'd seen Travis wearing last year, which meant it was probably something cool eighth-graders wore. His hair was all gelled up into a messy-yet-somehow-also-neat style, and on his feet were some crisp new shoes. "You look very nice today," I told him.

"Thanks."

"I wonder what classes we'll have. I hope we have all our classes together. Wouldn't that be so awful if we weren't in any of the same classes? I hope we have at least some of them together." Daniel and I had been in the same elementary school classes for kindergarten, second grade, third grade, and sixth grade. But even when we weren't in the same classes, we always played together at recess. In junior high, you don't get recess, so not having any of the same classes would be a real tragedy. I didn't think we'd have to worry about that, though. Out of seven classes, surely we'd have at least

11

one that overlapped.

Daniel just shrugged. He wasn't very talkative that morning, which struck me as odd, since usually we could talk for hours about any random thing. Daniel could make a conversation about anything. But maybe he was still nervous about starting junior high school.

The bus pulled up and we got on. I pulled Daniel toward a seat in the middle of the bus. The middle of the bus was the best place to sit. You didn't have all the rowdy kids like you would in the back, but you didn't have the bus driver breathing down your neck and eavesdropping on everything you said like you would in the front either.

The bus had just started moving when I heard a perky "Hi!" behind me. I turned around and saw a girl I didn't recognize sitting in the seat right behind us. She was pretty, with wavy red hair and big brown eyes.

Daniel and I both said "Hi" back.

"I'm Madalaine," she said, bouncing in her seat. "What are your names?"

"Alanna," I told her.

"I'm Daniel," said Daniel.

"Alanna and Daniel. Nice to meet you guys! Are you excited about junior high school? I'm excited. I can't wait to meet all sorts of people! Would you believe that I just moved here over the summer? My old town had middle school starting in sixth grade. I was so happy to find out that it starts in seventh here, so I'm not the only new kid! We're all new to the school together! It'll be great!"

I could tell right away that Madalaine was the kind of person who would have a million friends. She just had that natural ability to put a smile on your face.

Daniel started making conversation with Madalaine, and I sat back and listened. I'm not that good at talking to people other than Daniel, Lacey, and Travis. I mean, I'm not shy or anything, but sometimes I just don't know what to say. Daniel, Lacey, and Travis have known me since I was born, practically, so they're used to me. I don't have to worry about what to say in front of them. But other people have all these *rules* about conversations, like about when to give the other person a chance to talk, and what's okay to say to someone you just met, and what kind of comments would be considered totally random and out of place. I tend to make a lot of random and out of place comments, so I didn't want to open my mouth and make Madalaine think I was weird or something. Especially because she and

Daniel seemed to be getting along so great.

Madalaine and Daniel chatted the entire way to school. I didn't talk at all. We arrived at school and the bus dropped us off. We already knew we were supposed to go into the auditorium first thing, so the principal could welcome us to the school and go over rules and stuff. Daniel and I both knew where the auditorium was, because we'd seen Lacey in the school play last year, and the auditorium was where the play had been held. Madalaine didn't know where the auditorium was, so she just followed us. Or rather, she followed Daniel, because Daniel said, "I know where the auditorium is. Follow me."

As we walked, Daniel pointed certain things out—the library, the cafeteria, certain teachers' classrooms. Madalaine was impressed. "Wow, you already know your way around and everything! How do you know where everything is?"

"My brother went here last year, so I've been here for events and stuff. And we had push-up day last year too, where all the sixth graders from the elementary schools got to come here and take a tour."

"Oh. Lucky. So all you guys have, like, an advantage, 'cause you've already been here."

Daniel shrugged. "It's not too much of an advantage. You'll learn your way around pretty soon, I'm sure. Travis said he was really confused his first couple days here, but by like the second week he knew his way around."

"Is Travis your brother?"

"Yeah. He's in high school now. Freshman."

"Do you have any other brothers or sisters?"

"Nope. Just me and him." Daniel didn't add that he practically had two sisters as well, and that one of them was walking right next to him. "What about you? You have any brothers or sisters?"

"One of each. They're both younger than me, though. My brother's in third grade and my sister's in first."

Daniel and Madalaine chatted all the way to the auditorium. By the time we found a row of empty seats to sit down in, they knew all about each other's families, elementary schools, and interests. Daniel and I knew that Madalaine liked cupcakes, horses, and swimming, that she was from a small town in California, and that she was hoping to join a photography or yearbook club this year. Madalaine knew what I'd known for years— that Daniel had played soccer, baseball, and basketball at

15

various points in his life, that he liked the *Diary of a Wimpy Kid* books, and that his favorite food was butter crunch ice cream. I also learned a few new things about Daniel—like that he apparently thought photography and yearbook sounded really cool, and that he'd been considering joining a swim team. Interesting coincidences, huh?

Madalaine did not learn anything about me. Because I did not talk—how could I, with Daniel and Madalaine carrying on their two-sided conversation and always answering each other's questions without even giving me the chance to think about something I might want to say—and because Daniel did not even mention me when he was telling Madalaine about his life.

I kind of lost track of the conversation once we sat down. I stared around at all the kids pouring into the auditorium. These weren't just the kids from our old elementary school. These were kids from *all* the upper elementary schools across the city—all seven of them. Most of the kids were kids I didn't know. I was glad to have Daniel next to me, even though he hadn't said a word to me since the bus stop.

Once everyone was sitting down, or at least walking along the aisles with teachers *trying* to get them to sit down, the principal went up onstage and announced that it was time to be quiet and listen. The principal was Mr. Ducey. I heard Daniel whispering to Madalaine about how Mr. Ducey was a nice guy, but really, *really* strict about things like the dress code and swearing in the hallway. Stuff he'd learned from Travis and Lacey, obviously.

Mr. Ducey gave a speech welcoming all of us to the new school. He went over some rules, and talked about how the schedule went, and reminded everyone that they should make sure they know how they're getting home every day (car, walking, or bus). Then he announced that the teachers were going to be handing out schedules by alphabetical order according to last names, and it was time for all the students with last names A–C to head over to the double doors and receive their schedules. "Ohp, that's me," said Madalaine. "I'm C for Carson. Hey, it was great talking with you, Daniel. I hope we have some classes together."

"Yeah, me too," said Daniel.

And then, even though I'd sat there like a lump the entire time both in the auditorium and the bus, walking through the halls like Daniel's shadow and never saying a word, Madalaine turned to me and gave me a warm smile. "It was nice to meet you too. I hope you're in some of my classes. Well, have a nice day!"

"You too," I returned her smile and hoped she knew I was being sincere. Like I said, I'm not shy, and I actually have a lot to say—when people give me the chance to talk. Hopefully Madalaine and I *would* have some classes together, and I'd be able to tell her all about myself. So she'd know I was an actual human being with my own set of memories and likes and dislikes, not just Daniel's shadow.

My group was called next. D–G. "I'll wait for you," I told Daniel. Daniel's last name is Malone, so it'd be a while before he got to get his schedule. But I didn't mind waiting.

The lady giving out the schedules had curly gray hair that puffed all out around her head. It reminded me of a storm cloud, like a big cumulonimbus cloud about to burst and pour rain everywhere. A couple years ago, I would've blurted that out to her, but now I know that's the kind of thing I should really only say to Daniel and Travis and Lacey. I made a mental note to mention it to them later. They'd get a kick out of that, especially Travis. I figured the schedule lady—her ID read *Mrs. Tavery*—would not get a kick out of it.

"What's your name, sweetie?" Mrs. Tavery asked me.

"Alanna Fenn," I told her.

"Alanna Fenn… are you by any chance related to Lacey Fenn?"

"Yep. She's my sister. She's in high school now."

"I know, I had her in my literacy class last year. One of my best students." She looked down at my schedule. "You have Mr. Marks as your literacy teacher. Oh, you'll like him. He's very good."

I took my schedule, slightly relieved that I wouldn't have Mrs. Tavery as my literacy teacher. She seemed perfectly nice and everything, but, well, she'd had Lacey in her class. Lacey was the queen of anything academic. She could get good grades without even trying. As for me, I wasn't dumb or anything, but school didn't come as easily for me as it did for Lacey. I got okay grades, but I had to really work for them.

I went over to the double doors leading out of the auditorium. I stood right on the inside of the room, next to the door but so that I still had a clear view of the students crowding down near the stage. Daniel was still at his seat. His group hadn't been called yet.

"Did you already get your schedule?" a tall woman

with curly brown hair asked me. I nodded. "Then you can go out the doors and to your homeroom class. The teachers are expecting you guys. They'll tell you what to do next."

"I'm waiting for my friend," I told her. "His last name begins with M."

"Well, that's very nice that you're waiting for your friend, but everybody needs to go straight to their homeroom. If we get a bunch of students congregating around the doors waiting for their friends, it'll get really crowded here and nobody will be able to get out."

I moved to the outside of the double doors, in the hallway. The brown-haired lady shook her head. "Go to your homeroom class. You'll see your friend at lunch. If he asks where you went, I'll let him know you wanted to wait for him."

I scowled as I looked down at my schedule to see where my homeroom was. Room 36. I knew how the school was set up—single and double-digit numbers on the bottom floor, numbers in the hundreds on the middle floor, and numbers in the two-hundreds on the top floor. Of course, there weren't three hundred classrooms in the school. Each floor's numbers only went up into the 40s.

I purposely dawdled as I followed the signs to room 36, hoping Daniel would eventually catch up to me. But he didn't. He didn't show up in my homeroom class either. *Oh well,* I thought. *We're bound to have at least a couple of our classes together.*

But if there was one thing I was learning so far in junior high, it was that things didn't always go the way I wanted them to.

Chapter 3

Teams

At Finewood Junior High School, students were arranged into "teams". You were with your team for all five of your core classes: math, literacy, English, science, and social studies. The same exact group of kids, class after class, just like in elementary school. The only classes you got with other kids were your two UAs, or Unified Arts, which was basically a fancy word for "specials." Your UAs switched every trimester, so in one year you'd get six of them. Mine for this first trimester were art and FCS, which stood for Family and Consumer Science, which was basically a cooking and sewing class.

It really stunk having my five core classes with all the same kids. Well, it wouldn't have stunk if Daniel was on my team. But he wasn't. I was on team 7-2, and he was on team 7-4. Poo.

I figured that at least if Daniel wasn't on my team, he would be in one of my UAs. But when I went to art in the morning, he wasn't there. A few kids I knew from elementary school were there, but I didn't want to talk to any of them. It didn't feel right without Daniel.

I was so relieved when it came time for lunch. I spotted Daniel right away. I fought my way over to him through the pushing, yelling crowd. "Daniel!"

Daniel had been standing by a table, talking to someone. He turned around when he heard me yell his name. "Hey Alanna."

I joined him at the table. "What UA do you have seventh period?" I asked, first thing.

"Music. What about you?"

"GRRRR!" I yelled it a little too loudly. Students from surrounding tables turned to stare at me. "Poo. I have FCS."

"So do I!" a cheery voice peeped up from the other side of Daniel. It was only then that I realized that the person he'd been talking to was Madalaine. "I have FCS seventh period. Do you have Mrs. Haller?"

I pulled my schedule out of my pocket and consulted it. "Yep."

"Me too!" Madalaine held up her hand for a high five, and I slapped it. "That's awesome. I have FCS with you, and all of my core classes with Daniel."

What?! *Not* fair! Why did *Madalaine* get to be on Daniel's team? Why couldn't *I* be the one who shared all of Daniel's core classes? Madalaine got to see *my* best friend five periods a day, and I wasn't with him for a single stinking class.

Daniel sat down, so Madalaine and I sat down as well, one on either side of him. I remembered what I had wanted to tell him in the morning, about the teacher with the storm cloud hair. I turned to him. "Hey, Danie—"

His name wasn't even fully out of my mouth before Daniel turned to Madalaine. "That was so funny, second period, when that kid knocked his pencil case down and it made that big crash."

"Yeah!" Madalaine laughed. "And Mr. Brett jumped like a mile, and everyone was like, 'Oh my gosh, what was *that*?'"

They got into a conversation about their classes, and I was out of the loop because, oh yeah, I wasn't *in* any of their classes. None of the ones they had together, anyway.

I ate my lunch without saying much of anything. Then the bell rang, and Daniel and Madalaine had to go off to their literacy class together, and I had to go to my math class. "I'll see you in FCS," Madalaine said to me. She paused. "Sorry, I'm bad with names. What's your name again?"

"Alanna," I told her.

"Alanna. Right. I'll remember that! OK, well, I'll see you in FCS, Alanna."

Math was boring. So was English, which I had after math. Seventh period was FCS. I was a little late because I couldn't find the room at first, but apparently so was half the class. When I finally found the room and went inside, I had to refrain from gasping.

It was unlike any other classroom I'd ever been in. It actually resembled a kitchen more than a classroom. It was big and open, with all sorts of ovens and countertops, microwaves and toaster ovens, a refrigerator, several sewing machines, and large tubs of what looked like fabric. Despite the bad mood I'd been carrying around all day since finding out that Daniel and I weren't on the same team, a smile came to my face. I got the feeling that I was going to like this class.

"Alanna!" I looked toward the sound of my name and saw Madalaine waving to me from a table. The tables were interesting too—they looked more like kitchen tables than school desks. I walked over and sat next to Madalaine. "I imagine you three all know each other already," Madalaine said, motioning to me and the two girls sitting across from us.

I knew one of the girls from elementary school. "Hi Shelly," I said. She said hi back. I didn't know the other girl.

"This is Amanda," Shelly introduced me to the girl next to her. Amanda and I said hi to each other.

"How do you like junior high so far?" Shelly asked me.

I shrugged. "It's okay." Except for not having Daniel in any of my classes.

"It's different from elementary school," said Amanda. We all agreed.

Class started, and one of the first things the teacher said was that we were going to pick groups that we'd be in for the entire trimester. These would be our groups for anytime we cooked anything, since there weren't enough cooking appliances for each student to use their own.

"You can have three or four people in a group," Mrs. Haller said. "I'll let you choose your own groups unless there's any trouble. If you're having a hard time finding a group, let me know."

Madalaine looked around the table at Shelly, Amanda, and me. "Group?" she suggested. "The four of us?"

We all nodded. "It's weird how we're picking groups the first day. Like, before we really get to know anyone," Amanda commented.

"Maybe that's the point," I said. "Maybe she doesn't want people to have really good friends yet in the class, because then there'd be all these little cliques and people would get left out."

"Good point," said Amanda.

Mrs. Haller passed around a sheet of paper and asked one person from each group to write down the names of everyone in the group. Shelly wrote down the names for our group. Now we were a team.

The class wasn't all that interesting, because it was just the first day. Mrs. Haller went over the rules of the

Chapter 4

Home

Daniel finally boarded the bus, right before it was about to leave. By that time, Madalaine and I had taken seats together. It had been Madalaine's idea. I'd wanted to wait and sit with Daniel, but the bus was filling up quickly, and she suggested that we sit together so we didn't get stuck with bad seats. So I sat down next to her, even though the whole time I was still watching the door to see when Daniel would arrive.

When he did arrive, he was with a boy I didn't know. Daniel and the boy I didn't know were talking together, laughing like they'd been friends for years. But they hadn't been friends for years. I knew that, because if Daniel had been friends for years with someone, I would know him too. And I would have been friends for years with the same person.

As Daniel started walking through the aisle, I realized I didn't know what I was going to do when he came to my row. It would be a little rude to tell Madalaine to get up and find a new seat so Daniel could sit with me. But it would also be rude to tell Daniel, "Sorry, you can't sit with me. You snooze, you lose, bucko!" Of course, I could get up and offer Daniel my seat, but then *I'd* have to find a new place to sit, and that would defeat the whole purpose.

But Daniel didn't even make it to my row. Three seats behind the bus driver, there were two empty seats together, and Daniel and his new friend took them. Daniel turned around and waved to me and Madalaine. We waved back.

And we drove home that way. It was my very first school bus ride sitting next to someone other than Daniel. There had been days, during our elementary school years, when Daniel had been sick or had stayed home from school for other reasons (like one time, his uncle from Guatemala came for a one-day visit on the way to somewhere else, and Daniel and Travis got to stay home

31

from school so they could see him). But on those days, the seat next to me had remained empty.

It was weird sitting with Madalaine. When Daniel and I sat together, sometimes we talked, and other times, we just rode home silently. We didn't need to say anything. It was a comfortable silence.

With Madalaine, I felt like I needed to say something, but I didn't really know what. I just sat there, trying to think of something to say that wouldn't make me sound like a complete weirdo, until Madalaine asked me, "So, how do you like your classes?"

Glad to have something to talk about, I made a see-saw motion with my hand and said, "They were okay. Not too interesting, though."

"Yeah. They'll probably get more interesting later on. I guess the first day always has to be about rules and stuff."

We were able to talk for the rest of the ride home about classes, and then we arrived at Daniel's and my stop. "Bye," I said to Madalaine before I left.

"Bye Alanna. See you tomorrow." Madalaine then raised her voice. "Bye Daniel! See you tomorrow!"

Daniel turned around and smiled, waving to Madalaine. Then he and I walked off the bus.

"Well!" I said as the bus pulled away. "I'm glad *that* day's over. Only one hundred seventy-nine left to go!"

Daniel laughed. "Hey, it wasn't too bad. I think I'm really gonna like junior high. Did your homeroom teacher tell you about all the clubs they have? I think they have even more than they did last year. And the kids are nicer than I thought they'd be. You know, Travis and Lacey told us all the horror stories. I bet they were just trying to scare us."

"Who were you sitting next to on the bus?"

"Hunter. He's in my music class. Well, and my core classes. He was telling me about this cool computer program his dad has, where you can, like, design things, and then print them out on a 3D printer. It sounds really cool." We strolled down the road to where our two houses sat, right next to one another. "Where do you think Travis and Lacey'll be, your house or my house?"

"Or right here!" Lacey came running out of the backyard, followed by Travis. "You guys just had your first day of junior high! How was it?"

Daniel started rambling about how awesome it was, and I stayed quiet. I didn't really have anything to add other than that it had been boring and how awful it was that Daniel wasn't in any of my classes. Another thing

Chapter 5

A Pact

The second week into junior high, Daniel joined an after-school programming club with his new friend Hunter. I didn't even know he'd joined the club until he didn't show up on the bus on the way home. I asked Madalaine if she knew where he was and she told me. *Really*, Daniel? I knew he had all his classes with Madalaine, but he at least still ate lunch with me. Well, sort of. He could have told me then, or at home or something.

I say that Daniel "sort of" ate lunch with me, because it's true. The second day of junior high, I found Daniel at a table with Madalaine, Hunter, and some other kids from their classes. They made room for me at the table, but not in their conversation. I didn't get a chance to say a word. And that's how lunch had been continuing ever since.

Our parents and Travis and Lacey kept bugging Daniel and me about how we liked junior high. Daniel always responded enthusiastically that he loved it, that he was making so many new friends and having such a great time in his classes and getting interested in so many new things. I always responded with, "Meh." But by the time Daniel joined the programming club at the end of the second week, I had a very strong opinion about junior high. An opinion that I couldn't share with anyone unless I wanted them to think I was crazy.

Junior high *stunk*.

There was nothing good about it. I only got to see Daniel for twenty-six minutes a day (barely), the teachers were still trying to learn all our names and things about us, and the work was already starting to become hard. In only the second week.

The only part of junior high that I liked was my FCS class. Not so much the class itself—it was boring because we hadn't yet started cooking anything; we were still learning how to use all the equipment. But I liked my table group: Madalaine, Amanda, and Shelly. Madalaine just had that personality that could turn even the most rotten day into a good one. She always greeted me with a smile, always seemed excited to see me even when I couldn't imagine why. And, I was pleasantly surprised to find out, she and the other girls at our table were as easy to talk to as Daniel or Lacey or Travis. They didn't even care when I said something totally random.

So that's why, right when Amanda finished telling us all about something her cat did the other night, I butted my way into the conversation without worrying about whether somebody else was going to say something. "Does anyone know when programming club meets? Or where it is or when it starts or, like, anything about it?"

"I know it's gotta be some sort of computer club," said Shelly, laughing a little. "That's all I know about it."

"So it probably meets in the computer lab," Amanda deduced logically.

"But does anyone know *when* it meets?" I hadn't seen Daniel at all the day before. I'd watched his house from the moment I got home, waiting to see him walk up the front step. But he didn't get home until after five. By that time, Mom was calling me down for dinner, and even when I said it was *really important* that I talk with Daniel *right now*, she still made me eat my dinner first. And then, by the time I actually did get to go over to Daniel's house, his whole family had left. Lacey told me they'd gone out to eat.

I'd planned to ask Daniel about programming club on the bus ride to school, but *apparently* he'd had his dad drive him to school early so he could help Hunter with some project. I found all this out by listening to my table's conversations at lunch, but I didn't have a chance to talk to Daniel during lunch because he was sitting two seats away and spent the entire period talking to Madalaine and Hunter and his other new "friends".

I felt like a nobody.

But now, in FCS class, I wasn't a nobody. I was part of a group. And I had just started a conversation.

"I have no idea when it meets," said Amanda. "I didn't even know there *was* a programming club."

"Same," said Shelly. "Are you thinking about *joining* programming club? I never knew you were a computer geek."

"I'm not," I said. "But Daniel joined programming club, so I want to join too."

"Hey, so what's the deal with you and this Daniel kid?" asked Amanda. "You mention him all the time. Are you guys, like, dating or something?"

I shook my head. I was about to explain how we were best friends, and how even though we weren't dating *yet*, we still planned to marry each other when we grew up. But Madalaine started speaking before I got the chance.

"They're not dating," she explained. "They're just, like, super BFFs. They live next door to each other and grew up together and everything, kind of like a brother and sister."

I nodded, pleased that Madalaine understood so perfectly. Pleased that she remembered what I'd told her the first day of school.

"That's so cool," said Amanda. "I wish I had a best friend who lived next door to me." A thoughtful expression came over her face. "What's it like having a boy best friend?"

I'd never really thought about it before. With Travis and Lacey and Daniel and I, gender had never really mattered much. I'd never thought much about the fact that Daniel was a boy and I was a girl. He was just my best friend, not my *boy* best friend.

I shrugged. "I've never had a girl best friend, so I don't know how it compares," I said. "But, you know, we always have a lot of fun together, and stuff."

"It would be hard for me," Shelly admitted. "'Cause with a boy and a girl, there's always that—that *thing* in between, you know? Like, that knowledge that maybe he has a crush on you, or maybe you have a crush on him, or even if nobody has a crush right now, sometime in the future one of you might get a crush on the other, or he might start dating some girl, and you might get jealous... or he might start dating some girl and *she* might be jealous of *you*, 'cause she thinks there's something going on between you and him... or if you get a boyfriend, *he* might get jealous of your best friend, or your best friend might be jealous of him, and uggghhhhh, there's just too much drama. That's why I like just being friends with girls."

Madalaine started laughing. "Oh yeah, girls are sooooooo undramatic. You'll never have any drama at all if you only hang out with girls." She rolled her eyes. "I mean, come on. Girls cause most of the drama in rela-

41

tionships anyway. Even with friendships, same thing. Guys'll be like, 'Hey dude, you ticked me off,' and they'll punch each other a couple times and then the next day they'll be all buddy-buddy again. Girls hold onto stuff. Girls get jealous, and hold grudges."

We all looked around the table at each other. "You know what, we should make a pact," said Amanda. "The four of us girls, right here and now. We should make a pact that we won't get jealous of each other and we won't hold grudges. And we won't start hating each other's guts if we all fall for the same boy."

"That's a good idea," said Madalaine. "But I want to add something else. We should all agree not to go out with a boy who any of the others of us already have dibs on."

"Ooooh, yeah," said Shelly, her eyes wide. "Good one, Madalaine."

"Anyone have anything else to add?" asked Amanda. None of us did.

"All right," said Madalaine. "Let's pinky swear on it." She held out her pinkies to me and Amanda, and Amanda and I held our other pinkies out to Shelly, so the four of us were locked in a chain. And we made our pact.

Chapter 6
A Chat

That day, hurrah hurrah, I finally got to talk to Daniel. Not on the bus—Daniel sat with Hunter on the bus, so I sat with Madalaine. But when we got off at our bus stop, I finally, *finally* had my best friend all to myself.

"Your house or my house?" I asked as the bus pulled away.

"Yours," said Daniel. "That way I won't have to bother with my key."

All throughout our elementary school years, Mrs. Malone had been a stay-at-home mom. Just like my mom, she'd been home every day when we left for school, and when we got back from school. After school, Daniel and I hadn't really cared where we hung out. We would go to his house for the Wii and the tree fort and my house for the 72-inch TV and the swing set. But this year, with Travis in high school and Daniel in junior high, Mrs. Malone had decided it was time for her to go back to work. Not part time like my mom worked, but full-time. This year both of Daniel's parents got home around 5:30, and until that time, they had a strict rule that the doors had to be locked. Travis and Daniel could unlock the doors to go in when they got home, and then they had to lock them again. It was a major pain in the butt, so we'd been hanging out mostly at my house for the past few weeks.

As we strolled down the road, I turned to Daniel to ask him about programming club. But he asked me a question first. "Hey, so, uh, you hang out with Madalaine, right?"

I shrugged. "Not as much as you hang out with her," I said, hoping he'd catch what I wasn't saying—that it should have been *me* in all his classes, not Madalaine. "She's in my FCS class and I always end up sitting with her on the bus because you sit with Hunter." *Hint,*

hint, you should be sitting with me. "Why were you asking?"

"Um," Daniel said, looking away. "Just wondering, does she, uh… does she ever mention me?"

Why do you want to know? My mind went on defensive. "Why do you care?" I asked, a little more rudely than I meant to.

"I don't. I'm just asking."

"Why would you ask if you don't care?"

Daniel gave me a disbelieving look. "What's *up* with you today? Why are you being so…so snappy, or whatever? I just asked a question!"

I couldn't put into words how I felt. And suddenly I realized that maybe Daniel's question really had been just a question.

"I'm sorry," I muttered. "It's just…this whole junior high thing is new to me, you know? The stress is kind of getting to me." He was still waiting for an answer to his question, so I said grudgingly, "And yes, Madalaine does talk about you." *Not as much as I talk about you, though.*

"She does? What does she say?"

Again, why was he so eager to know? "She talks about stuff you guys did in your classes," I said carefully.

"And, well, sometimes I mention you, so…yeah."

"What kind of stuff do you say about me?"

I shrugged. "Just that you're my best friend and some of the fun stuff we've done together. Race you home!" I took off running. Running away from Daniel's questions about Madalaine.

Lacey was waiting for us when we got to my house. Just Lacey. Well, and Mom, but no Travis. "Where's Travis?" I asked accusingly.

"How about, 'Oh hi Mom, hi Lacey, how nice to see you'?" suggested Mom.

"Well, that too, but *where's Travis?*"

"At his house," replied Lacey, who was hunched over her laptop. "He lives there, you know."

Duh. But it was unsettling, the fact that Travis was at his house and Lacey was at hers. It was a weekday afternoon. This was our time to hang out together, all four of us, or at least in our best friend pairs.

"What's Travis doing at home?" I asked Lacey.

"How should I know?"

"Did you guys get in a fight?" I thought about how close Daniel and I had been to getting in a fight and wondered, *what the heck is wrong with this year?*

But Lacey shook her head. "No, I just have a lot of

homework for my AP class. I told him I wouldn't be able to hang out today, so he decided to go home. Now, if you'll excuse me, now that *you're* home I'm going to move this workstation to my room." She picked up her laptop and the various papers she had scattered across the kitchen table and left the room.

"That looked like a lot of homework for the second week of school," Daniel commented.

"Yeah, well, that's what you get if you sign up for an AP class," I told him. Lacey had proudly informed me that AP classes were usually reserved for juniors and seniors, and maybe a few ambitious sophomores. But the AP World History class at Lacey's high school was available for freshmen as well, so of course Lacey had chosen to take it.

"Remind me never to sign up for an AP class," said Daniel, and we both laughed, and everything seemed back to normal.

That is, until I remembered my question for Daniel. "Hey, I've been meaning to ask you," I said, as we rummaged through the pantry for a snack. "When does programming club meet?"

"Tuesdays and Thursdays from three to six, why?"

"Three to *six*? That's a long time."

"Yeah, but you kinda need that long for some of the projects we're gonna be working on. We're gonna make robots! Well, later in the year anyway. First we gotta learn all the basic stuff."

Making a robot seemed kind of cool. "So, after we learn the basic stuff, does it turn into, like, a robot making club? Do we get to start making robots every day?" I imagined what it would be like to have a bunch of robots, one for each chore I needed to do. "That sounds so cool!" I laughed. "By the end of the year, we'll have a robot for everything! One to clean our rooms, one to brush our teeth, one to cook dinner for our families, one to do our homework, one to, I don't know, comb our hair or something…"

Daniel laughed too. "Dream on. We're going to make *one* robot over the course of the year, and it's not going to be able to do stuff like that. The most it'll be able to do is walk and turn around and maybe pick something up."

"Only *one* robot for the whole year?" That didn't sound very interesting. "What are we going to *do* from three to six every day? It can't take *that* long just to build one robot who doesn't even do anything."

Daniel grabbed a bag of chips and sat down at the kitchen table. I followed him, carrying a package of shortbread cookies. Daniel grabbed a cookie from my package and started chewing. "First of all," he said, opening the bag of chips. "I don't know why you keep saying *we*. *You're* not in programming club."

"But I'm going to be."

Daniel laughed like he couldn't believe it. "Are you kidding? *Why?* You don't know anything about programming. You've never been interested in programming like I have."

He was right. Mr. Malone was a software engineer, so Daniel and Travis practically grew up learning to program. I didn't, and I never had an interest. But I wanted to be with Daniel.

"I could learn easily," I said, even though I wasn't sure. "And it's not like I have *no* experience. I like going on the computer and stuff."

"Yeah, to watch YouTube."

"So?"

"So YouTube has nothing to do with programming. Unless you watch programming videos. Which you don't. You listen to Taylor Swift and watch funny animals."

"Okay, but I could *learn* to program."

Daniel just shook his head. "Alanna, find something that interests *you*. Programming is what interests *me*. Join a club that you can be excited about."

"I can be excited about hanging out with you. No matter what we're doing."

"Well..." Daniel looked a little uncomfortable. "Look, we're best friends. We know that. Everybody knows that. But best friends don't have to like all the same things and do all the same things. I think it's time we start branching out a little. Finding our own interests. Figuring out what we want to do with our lives."

What we want to do with our lives? I already knew what I wanted to do with my life. What we all wanted to do with our lives. We'd planned it out, seven years ago. I was going to marry Daniel.

Beyond that, I didn't really know anything else.

Chapter 7

Basketball

I didn't join programming club. Honestly, I didn't really *want* to spend three whole hours every Tuesday and Thursday sitting in front of a computer or working on a tiny little piece of a robot or whatever else they did in programming club. But that left me with a three-hour space two days a week in which it would be impossible to hang out with Daniel. What in the world was I going to do?

Before I knew it, it was Tuesday, and Daniel was at programming club. The bus ride home wasn't bad, because I rode with Madalaine, and we talked the entire time about something funny that had happened in our

FCS class. But as soon as I got off at my bus stop, I felt alone. And lonely.

It was ridiculous. Junior high had just started barely three weeks ago, and already it was my second time walking home from the bus stop alone. I remembered the few times in elementary school when Daniel had been absent, and how long and boring the walk home from the bus stop had always seemed without him. It was the same way now, just longer, because the junior high bus stop was farther away than our old elementary school one.

At least one thing was right by the time I got home. Travis and Lacey were both in the living room, studying together. I stood there in the doorway for a moment, just watching the two of them. It was a sweet picture. They made such a good couple. The only thing that would make the image better would be if they'd move a little closer together on the couch. Then maybe Travis could put his arm around Lacey, and she could kind of lean against him, and they could study that way, cuddled up together.

That's what they'll look like studying in a couple months, I told myself. Now that they were in high school, it wouldn't be long before they officially started dating.

I must have made some sort of noise, because Travis suddenly looked up and saw me. He stood up. "Hi Alanna," he said. "How was school today?"

I shrugged. "School."

"Yeah," Travis shrugged too. "Same here."

"What are you guys studying?" I asked.

"Oh, Lacey was just helping me with my algebra homework. You know, since she's that brilliant genius who took algebra *last* year," said Travis, grinning at Lacey. "Now she has to do her brilliant genius homework for her AP class, and I was just getting ready to head out and play some basketball in my driveway."

What? So Travis and Lacey *weren't* planning on spending the whole afternoon together? How were they ever going to date if they didn't even spend their afternoons together?

I was so disgruntled by this fact that I missed Travis saying something. "I'm sorry, what?"

"Wanna come?" Travis was looking at me. "I mean, I know Daniel's still at school, so if you wanted something to do, you could come shoot some hoops with me. Only if you want to."

Shooting hoops with Travis sounded better than moping around at home or watching Lacey do her homework. "Sure," I said.

Travis and I walked next door, and he typed the code into the keypad next to the garage door. There were all sorts of security measures at the Malone house now that both parents were at work. Travis went into the garage and came out with a basketball. "So, you wanna play HORSE or something? Or we could just shoot around, or whatever."

"HORSE is good."

"You wanna start?"

I took a shot from the edge of the driveway and made it. Travis and I both looked at each other, surprised that it had gone in. "Nice shot, Alanna!" he exclaimed. "Way to start off the game!"

"Thanks." I smirked. "Now you have to make the same shot."

Travis missed. He's a basketball player—he's played since seventh grade. But he missed the shot that I'd made. He made a face at me. "Okay, show-off, let's see if you can sink another one."

I stood over by the mailbox and shot. The ball bounced off the backboard…and into the basket. Again, Travis and I exchanged disbelieving glances. "Are you some sort of basketball prodigy or something?" Travis asked.

I laughed. "Yes. Obviously." He knew I wasn't. We'd played basketball before, me and Daniel versus Travis and Lacey, and Travis was by far the best. I'd always been able to make some good shots, but I wasn't great or anything. These were just lucky shots.

Travis made the mailbox shot, but it was still my turn to lead. I stepped off the driveway and took a few steps backward into the yard. I shot again, and this time the ball bounced off the rim and didn't go in. I shrugged. "Oh well, even prodigies make mistakes."

We kept playing. The game lasted for a while because we were pretty even, but finally I won, giving Travis the E by sinking a basket from halfway into my yard. "I never knew you were so good at basketball," Travis commented.

"Me neither," I said, shrugging. "Maybe it's my height." I had grown a couple inches over the summer, which was actually super annoying because I was now taller than Daniel. We'd always been the same height before. But I guess my tall-ness had an advantage when it came to shooting baskets.

"Have you thought about trying out for the basketball team? At Finewood?"

I hadn't. Of course I hadn't. I hadn't even known I was good at basketball until today. And, well, we hadn't really determined if I was good at *basketball*, just that I could make some cool shots. I shrugged. "I don't know what time they practice or anything. Maybe I'll check it out. I'll see if Daniel wants to do it with me."

"You and Daniel don't always have to do the same things, you know. Plus, you wouldn't even be doing it together, since you'd be on the girls' team and he'd be on the boys' team."

Travis was right. It was just so weird thinking about signing up for anything without Daniel, even though clearly he didn't think the same thing about signing up for something without me. "We'll have to find out how good I am at real basketball first," I said. "Maybe on Thursday? If Lacey's busy doing her boring homework again?"

"You want to come over again on Thursday? Yeah, sure! We can do that." Travis narrowed his eyes. "And this time, I'm gonna beat you."

I grinned. I'd found something to do while Daniel was at programming club. And although it wasn't ideal, although I'd still prefer to be hanging out with Daniel, playing basketball with Travis was at least a fun way to keep myself occupied during those long, boring stretches of time on Tuesdays and Thursdays.

Chapter 8

With and Without

The next day Daniel met me at the bus stop with a buzz cut. He'd had kind of long hair before that—not girly long, but long for a boy, down over his ears and stuff. I didn't know what to make of his new haircut. He'd never had it that short before.

"Hey Alanna," he said, like nothing was out of the ordinary.

"Hey," I said back to him, giving him a weird look. Then, since he still wasn't saying anything, I asked, "What's with the haircut?"

Daniel shrugged. "Just ready for a change, you know? I've worn my hair in the same style for, like, almost my entire life. I wanted something different." He grinned. "Maybe you should get your hair cut like mine."

Obviously, he was joking. I made a face anyway and said, "Nah... I'm good."

"Oh, but why not?" asked Daniel in mock surprise. "You always want to do everything else like me, so why not get the same haircut?"

It was just a teasing remark. But somehow, it hurt. *You always want to do everything else like me*, as if... as if he had a problem with it or something. We were best friends. I wanted to be *with* him, not to be *like* him. There was a difference.

I didn't get to say anything else, though, because the bus pulled up. We both got on and went to what had become our normal seats—Daniel toward the front next to Hunter, me in the middle next to Madalaine.

"Oh my gosh," Madalaine said softly as I sat down next to her. She craned her neck around to take another look at Daniel. "He cut his hair! Oh my... he looks so different now! Wow!" She turned back to me. "I think it looks good on him. I mean, he always looked good before too, but now you can really see his face and...wow. It's actually a pretty good look for him, don't you think?"

I didn't. Daniel's new buzz cut was just one more thing that had changed since elementary school. One more thing that separated him from the Daniel I'd always known, who'd always been my best friend.

And after school, Daniel dropped another bomb on me. We walked home from the bus stop together, and he just randomly turned to me and said, "Hey, so do you think you could help me make some posters? Maybe this weekend? I'm running for student council, and I want to put my name out *everywhere*. People will only vote for kids they've heard of, you know?"

"Student council?" I asked. Lacey had been on student council, but I couldn't remember whether that was one of the activities that met after school or whether it just met during school.

"Yeah, it's really cool, you get to meet with all the other student council members and plan dances and stuff. And just, like, cool things for the students to do."

That didn't sound too bad. "Is it after school or during school?"

"After school, usually on Mondays, sometimes also on Wednesdays. I was really hoping it wouldn't meet on Tuesdays or Thursdays, because of programming

60

club, and it doesn't! So I can be in it!"

"I can be in it too, right?" I asked.

Daniel paused. "Um…sorry, but all the applications had to be in today. Didn't you hear the announcements?"

The announcements. The ones at the beginning of the school day, right after the Pledge of Allegiance? Who ever listens to those? I couldn't remember what I'd been doing in homeroom, but I sure hadn't been paying attention to the announcements.

"Do you think they'd made an exception?" I asked meekly.

Daniel shook his head. "Probably not. They have a deadline for a reason. But even if you can't be in student council, you can still help *me* get into student council. We can make posters. That's something we can do together."

Yeah. Something we could do together, so that the result would be Daniel spending even more time away from me. "Isn't there some sort of club we could join together?" I asked.

Daniel looked at me sort of sadly. "Alanna… we're in junior high now. There are lots of different clubs and teams and things to belong to, for people with lots of different interests. You and I… well, we have different interests. We can still be friends at home, without doing everything together at school."

It sounded like Daniel was telling me he didn't want to be friends at school anymore. Like, at all. It sounded like he was breaking up with me or something, even though we weren't technically boyfriend and girlfriend yet. Could you break up with a friend?

I didn't care. I didn't want any more of the conversation. "Let's hang out with Travis and Lacey when we get home. Let's find something fun to do, all four of us."

"Yeah, sure." Daniel shrugged. "As I said, we can still hang out at home."

I didn't want just a home friendship. I wanted a real friendship, the way it had always been before. But I didn't say anything about it, because at least Daniel was agreeing to my suggestion.

Travis was playing basketball in his driveway when we arrived. "Hey, where's Lacey?" I greeted him just as he geared up for a shot.

He turned at the sound of my voice and the ball went flying way off to the side of the net. "Hey Alanna. Hey Daniel. What's up?"

"Where's Lacey?" I asked again.

"At your house, studying. You guys wanna shoot

some hoops with me?"

"Nah," Daniel responded, at the same time I said, "Sure." Daniel and I looked at each other. "We don't have to," I said quickly.

"Oh, come on, little brother," said Travis. "You're just scared Alanna'll whip your butt. This girl has some *talent*!"

I couldn't help smiling a little.

Daniel shrugged. "Whatever. We can play for a little while, but then I want to do something else."

We played HORSE. Travis won, but I ended the game with only H-O. Daniel lost.

"I'm done," he said when the game was over. "What do you guys want to do now?"

Travis and I looked at each other. I kind of wanted to continue playing basketball. But we'd done what I wanted to do; now it was time to do something Daniel wanted to do. "I don't know," I said. "You pick something."

"Wii?" he suggested.

"Okay." I followed Daniel toward the house. We'd reached the front door by the time I realized Travis had resumed shooting hoops.

"Are you coming?" I asked him.

He looked over and hesitated. I could tell he was considering it. But he shook his head. "Nah, I'll stay out here. Gotta keep my shots hot so I can keep beating you!"

Disappointed, I followed Daniel into the house and to the living room, where the Wii was set up. But even as Daniel put the game in the console and handed me a remote, my mind couldn't help going back to the driveway. Travis liked playing Wii. He'd played in Wii championships with us before. Why didn't he want to play with us now? Maybe it was because Lacey wasn't here. Maybe it was weird for him, hanging out with just Daniel and me, and no Lacey. But he'd seemed to have fun playing HORSE with just Daniel and me.

This was ridiculous. I was with my best friend, just him and me, the way I'd wanted it to be ever since the school year started. Daniel was hanging out with me, just me, and all his conversations were directed toward me. The way it should be. It didn't matter that Travis had chosen to stay outside.

So why did I care so much?

Chapter 9

A Fight

Daniel went back to practically ignoring me when we returned to school the next day. He sat with Hunter and everybody on the bus, which I was getting used to. I had Madalaine, after all. Then at lunch, we still sat together at the same table, but I wasn't part of the conversation. Which I was also used to.

But it was what happened on Friday that I would have a hard time forgiving him for.

I was coming from my fifth period class—math— heading to my sixth period class, English. And suddenly, I saw Daniel in the hallway, walking with some kids I didn't know. He wasn't facing me, but I recognized the back of his head, with that stupid buzz cut. "Daniel!" I yelled excitedly. "Hi Daniel!"

Daniel didn't turn around. I knew I was risking being late for English, but figured it was more important to say hi to my best friend, since I hardly ever got to see him at school anymore. So I dashed through the hallway, dodging groups of students until I got to Daniel. I threw my arms around him from the back. "Hi Daniel," I said.

Daniel turned around. "What the—" he noticed it was me. "Alanna! What are you doing?"

"Just saying hi."

"That's not the way normal people say hi to each other."

For the first time, I noticed that Daniel's face was red. I'd embarrassed him! But how was getting a hug from your best friend embarrassing? I looked around and saw that the kids Daniel had been walking with were all staring at us. What was the big deal? They knew Daniel and I were friends, right?

"Do you know what people will think if they see you doing that?" Daniel asked me, frowning.

"That I haven't seen you in a really long time?" I asked.

66

"Worse than that. Alanna, this is junior high. Girls don't just randomly run up and hug guys unless they're, you know, going out together. People are going to think we're dating!"

"What's so bad about that?"

Daniel stared at me incredulously. *"What's so bad about that?* We're *not* dating! This is how rumors get started! You probably just started a rumor about us, just by doing what you just did."

The bell rang. My English class was starting. I figured Daniel was probably starting more of a rumor by standing here talking to me—no, more like *yelling* at me in the middle of the hallway, after the bell had rung, but I didn't say anything about that. "If people think we're dating, then so what?" I asked. "I mean, we will be eventually, so does it really matter?"

The kids around us started laughing. "I don't know, Dan, she's pretty into you," one guy commented. "Maybe you should just go out with her."

"Yeah, after all, if you will *eventually*, what does it matter?" another one teased.

Daniel's expression turned into the kind of scowl I'd only seen on him a few times before, usually when we were little and Travis was trying to boss him around. "Alanna, what did I tell you about talking to me at school? Just because we're neighbors doesn't mean you have to be my shadow. I have my own friends; maybe it's time for you to make your own friends. And no, we're *not* going to date eventually. We're just neighbors. That's it. Nothing more."

I felt like he'd slapped me. *Just* neighbors? Nothing more? Of course we were more than just neighbors. We were friends. Best friends. Maybe he wasn't ready to be "more than friends" quite yet, but that still didn't mean we were just neighbors.

A teacher came out of the classroom nearest to us. "Where should you kids be right now?" she asked.

"We're heading to class," one of Daniel's friends said. "Come on, guys."

Daniel turned around and walked off with his friends, without another glance at me. As they walked away, I heard one of them say, "So, Dan, looks like you've got yourself a *stalker*."

"I still don't get what's so bad about her stalking you, if you're going to be boyfriend and girlfriend *eventually*."

"Shut up," Daniel said.

"I don't know, she was pretty convinced! Are you *sure* she's just your neighbor?"

I'd heard enough. I turned and started walking toward my English class, trying to fight back the tears that were threatening to come out of my eyes. For the first time, I wished it were a Tuesday or a Thursday, so Daniel would have to go to programming club. Because I couldn't imagine walking home with him from the bus stop after he'd said all those hurtful things about me.

Somehow I made it through English. Then I went to FCS. "Something happened," Madalaine said immediately when I sat down. "What happened, Alanna?"

I couldn't believe she had noticed. I wasn't crying or anything. I'd managed to get control of myself before I'd even gone into English. How could Madalaine tell something was wrong?

I didn't want to talk about it, not even with my friends. Did this make Madalaine, Shelly, and Amanda my best friends now? I didn't think so. Even though they were more willing to be my friends than my *actual* best friend was, it took more than that to be a best friend. Best friends had a history together. Best friends had inside jokes and memories of a thousand good times.

I didn't have any of that with these girls, not yet. They were simply my friends.

"I'm okay," I told Madalaine. "Someone got mad at me before last period, but I'll get over it." This was how you had to act in junior high. You had to pretend things didn't bother you.

"Who?" Shelly leaned forward, her brown eyes wide. "Why did they get mad at you?"

"It's nothing," I said. I've always been a terrible liar, and I knew I wouldn't be able to keep pretending nothing was wrong if they kept pestering me about it. I'd break down and become a sobbing mess in the middle of FCS class—which would probably convince Mrs. Haller that I wouldn't be a good person to use the stove once we actually started cooking.

I needed a way to distract them, so I said the first thing that popped into my mind. "Hey, one of my friends said I should try out for basketball. What do you think?"

"Yeah!" Amanda exclaimed. "You should. I'm going to try out. We can be on the team together!"

"You're tall," Shelly added. "I know that helps a lot in basketball. That's about all I know about basketball." She giggled.

"Go for it," said Madalaine. "When are tryouts?"

"I have no idea."

"Well, find out!"

"Yeah. Maybe I will." If Daniel didn't want to be friends with me anymore, I'd need *something* to occupy my time.

"I'll ask my homeroom teacher," said Amanda. "She's been teaching here for like, thirty years, and I know she's into sports. I'll let you know."

"Okay." What had I just done? Had I just glued myself in to trying out for basketball? Of course, I hadn't actually signed up or anything, but Amanda seemed pretty excited about trying out for basketball with me. Did that mean I was going to do it?

Was I actually going to join my first after-school activity without Daniel?

Chapter 10

An Agreement

I woke up on Saturday annoyed that it was the weekend. Usually I liked weekends. At least, I did before I started junior high, because back then, weekends were entirely taken up with me, Daniel, Lacey and Travis doing fun things together. Not anymore. Last weekend, we'd spent a *little* bit of time together, but then Travis and Daniel had needed to go somewhere with their family. This weekend, I'd be lucky to get even a minute with Daniel. He'd be working on his posters for student council, and even if he had time to take a break from that, he was probably still mad at me. Mad at me for being his friend.

I stayed in bed until 11:57, because I knew I wouldn't have anything to do once I got up. At 11:57, Mom came into my room and exclaimed, "Alanna! What are you still doing in bed? You've slept half the day away!"

"It's the weekend," I told her.

"Well, I don't have a problem with you sleeping in for a couple hours on the weekend, but noon is ridiculous."

I got up. I went to the kitchen, where Lacey was sitting at the table, typing away on her laptop. "Why aren't you with Travis?" I grouched.

Lacey looked up. "Well, aren't you Little Miss Sunshine. What's the big deal with Travis? Why are you always asking about him?"

"I'm just wondering why he isn't with you."

Lacey rolled her eyes. "What are we, Siamese twins? Travis and I don't have to spend every minute together."

"But you used to."

"We used to be less busy. Maybe I should be asking you, where's Daniel?"

I opened my mouth, but no words came out. Finally, I sank into the chair across from Lacey and put my head down on the table. I could feel the tears coming, and there was nothing I could do to stop them.

"Alanna... what's wrong? Did you and Daniel get in a fight or something?"

I nodded. I couldn't bring myself to tell her about it. I didn't even want to think about it. I cried for a couple minutes into my arms, then picked my head up. Lacey was looking at me sympathetically.

"I don't want to talk about it," I said.

"Okay," she said. "But what are you going to do about it?"

I sniffled. "*Do* about it?"

"Well, you can sit here feeling miserable, or you can get up and fix your problem. Personally, I think fixing your problem would be a little more productive."

She was right. It would be a total waste of my day if I just sat and cried the whole time; I knew that. But how was I supposed to fix my problem? It wasn't even *my* problem, really. It was Daniel's. He was the one who didn't want to hang around with me anymore. How could I fix that?

A thought crept into my mind. Maybe there was one thing I could do. I knew where Daniel was at the moment—at his house, making posters for student council. I hadn't wanted to help with those because if he made it into student council, that would give him less time to spend with me. But if it was a choice between him not *having* a lot of time to spend with me and him not *wanting* to spend his time with me, I knew which one I'd choose. Helping Daniel with his posters would show him that I cared about him. It would show him that I supported his dreams, even when his dreams conflicted with mine. It would show him I was a friend worth keeping.

I stood up and wiped my eyes on my sleeve. "I'm going over to Daniel's house," I told Lacey.

"There you go." She smiled. "Good for you. Now you're solving your problem."

I couldn't believe the amount of courage it took just to walk next door, to my second home, basically, and ring the doorbell. And that in itself was weird, ringing the doorbell. Usually I'd just open the door to Daniel's house like it was my own, and he'd do the same at my house. But at a time like this, I felt it was most appropriate to ring the doorbell.

Travis answered the door. His face brightened into a smile when he saw me. "Alanna! Hey! Come in."

"Where's Daniel?" I asked.

"In his room, working on some project for school. I take it you're here to see him?"

I nodded and twisted my fingers together. Travis gave me an odd sort of look. "Are you okay? You seem kind of... nervous, or something."

"He might not want to see me. Just something that happened at school."

"Oh. Well..." Travis's face curled back into a smile. "If that happens, you could always come play basketball with me."

I couldn't help smiling just a little bit in return. "Okay. Hey, by the way, I might try out for the school team."

"Your school's basketball team? Awesome! Yeah, you totally should. You'd definitely make it. When are tryouts?"

"I don't know. I have a friend who's also going to try out. She's going to find out when they are."

"Sweet. Well, um, if you want to practice at all before then, you can, you know, come over any time."

I nodded. "I will." Wait, did that mean that I was definitely going to try out?

It didn't matter at the moment. What mattered was

that I needed to find Daniel and talk to him and help him with his posters. I started toward the stairs. "I'm going to go see if Daniel will talk to me."

"Yeah, go for it. I'm sure he will. He never stays mad for long."

I headed up the stairs and turned left at the landing. Daniel's door was closed. I knocked.

"Yeah?" Daniel's voice came from inside.

"Hi," I said, my heart pounding. "It's me. Alanna. Can I come in?"

Daniel didn't answer right away. I held my breath. "Yeah," he finally said.

I opened the door and stepped in. The floor was a mess. Daniel was sitting next to his bed, with a poster board in front of him. The floor was littered with four other poster boards, a bunch of construction paper scraps, various tape dispensers and markers, and containers of glue. "Nice posters," I said. "Looks like you're working hard on them." He had two posters done, and they really did look nice. But I was mainly just making conversation.

Daniel didn't say anything back; he just kept working on his posters. So I asked, "Can I help?"

Daniel nodded. "Use that one," he said, pointing to

the blank board closest to the door.

"What do you want me to write?"

"Just the kind of stuff I've been writing on my other ones. 'Daniel Malone for Student Council' and stuff like that. And then maybe 'strong leadership skills' or something like that, you know, to give a reason why people would want to vote for me."

"Okay." I selected a green marker—Daniel's favorite color—and started writing. We both worked silently for a while, and then Daniel said kind of gruffly, "Hey, so, I'm sorry about yesterday. Saying we weren't friends and stuff like that. I was just embarrassed."

I nodded. It still hurt, what he'd said and what he'd done. But the fact that he had just apologized made me feel a little better.

We kept working in silence, and then I got the courage to speak up. "I guess I don't get why you were embarrassed," I said. "All I did was hug you. I was happy to see you because I hadn't seen you much that day. It feels like we never see each other at school." I kept my gaze down on the poster I was creating. "I guess I just… don't really understand why being friends with me is embarrassing to you," I said quietly. Did I really want an answer?

Daniel sighed. "It's not… you," he said. "You're not really the problem. The problem is… well, other people don't understand about us. The kids we went to elementary school with do, but most of the people I've been hanging out with are people I just met this year. They don't know about how we've been friends since we were babies and stuff like that. So… when you're always trying to follow me around and do everything with me… it looks like you're my girlfriend. And people tease me about it. And people spread rumors. And I don't like it."

"But I still don't understand what's so awful about people thinking I'm your girlfriend. We're going to get married someday, right? You and me? And we're going to live next door to Travis and Lacey, and our kids will be best friends with their kids, and… right?"

"Alanna…" Daniel sighed again. "It's a long way off. I know that's what we all decided when we were little kids. But we were *little kids.* Sometimes…" he shrugged. "Sometimes, you know, stuff changes."

I suddenly felt very scared. *Stuff changes.* I knew that. Everybody knew that. Stuff had always been changing, ever since… well, ever since ever. But there were some things that were supposed to stay the same. Such as Daniel and me being best friends with each other, and our plans for when we grew up.

I didn't want to talk about it anymore. I held up the half-done poster. "What do you think? So far?"

"I think it looks good," said Daniel. "But maybe add some more colors. A border around the edge, or something like that."

"That's what I was going to do."

I started working on my border, and Daniel finished the poster he'd been working on and started a new one.

"You have friends at school, right?" Daniel asked, as I capped the orange marker I'd been using and picked up a blue one. "I mean, other than me?"

"Yeah," I said, surprised that he'd asked, and even more surprised that I was able to answer affirmatively. "I mean, I sit with Madalaine and Shelly and Amanda in FCS, and they're all really nice."

"Good," said Daniel. "Yeah, Madalaine told me she likes her FCS table. That's good."

I finished the border, and the poster was basically done. So I sat there, watching Daniel cut out bubble letters for his, and I tried to gather up the courage to ask him another question.

"So…" I finally said. "In school. You don't want me

to talk to you anymore? Is that it?"

"You can talk to me," Daniel said, tossing me a sheet of construction paper and a pair of scissors. "I mean, like, you can say hi to me in the halls and stuff. And obviously you can still eat lunch with us. But nothing overboard. No hugging or talking about how much you miss me or anything like that. And then we'll still hang out after school. Obviously. And on weekends, and yeah. I just don't want people to think stuff that isn't true. Like that we're dating."

"So you want us to be secret friends."

"Not *secret* exactly. Just... just not *best* friends. At school," he added quickly. "We'll still be best friends whenever we're at home. Okay? Is that a deal?"

And although I didn't like the way he phrased it— "Is that a deal?" like he was just trying to come to an agreement, and only wanted to be friends with me to keep *me* happy or not hurt my feelings or something, I nodded. Because I couldn't imagine a life without Daniel, and having him as a best friend after school and on weekends was better than not having him at all.

Chapter 11

Posters

Student council elections were all the rage the next week at school. Daniel's posters went up, and so did posters for about ten other kids. There were five slots available in student council for new kids. Everybody was out to win as many votes as they could.

Madalaine was running, although in FCS she told Shelly, Amanda and me that she felt kind of bad. "I mean, Daniel decided to run first," she said. "It was only *after* he told me about it that I decided it sounded like fun, and that I wanted to do it too. But... I mean, well, what if I end up taking votes away from him? I'd feel really bad if I made it and he didn't, since he was the one who got me interested in it in the first place."

"Madalaine," said Shelly. "You're way too nice."

"Yeah," agreed Amanda. "You really are. Don't worry about it. Let him worry about his campaign, and you worry about yours. Or you guys could help each other, and then both campaigns would be awesome."

I didn't want Madalaine helping Daniel with his campaign. The more people who helped him, the more likely he'd be to win. And I didn't want him to win, because I wanted him to be home more, so he could spend more time with me. Plus, I just didn't like the idea of Madalaine and Daniel spending any more time together than they already did. They had five of their classes together, and on top of that, they ate lunch together. Wasn't that enough?

"I already helped him with his campaign," I said. "I went over to his house on Saturday and we made some posters together."

"Oh, you helped with those? They look really nice!" exclaimed Madalaine. "I don't know, though. I still feel like I should do something for his campaign. Maybe I'll get some poster board tonight and make a couple posters."

And the next morning, on the bus, Madalaine was

holding three rolled-up posters. "Are those for your campaign?" I asked, hoping they were.

But she shook her head. "They're for Daniel's. Wanna see?"

I nodded grudgingly.

Madalaine glanced across the aisle, to where Daniel and Hunter were sitting several rows in front of us. It looked like Daniel was showing Hunter something—I couldn't tell what—so they weren't paying any attention to us. Madalaine unrolled the first poster.

In the center of the poster was a huge photo of Daniel. I had no idea where she'd gotten the picture, since even Daniel hadn't used pictures on his own posters. But it was definitely a picture of Daniel. Above it, in big, bold, 3D-looking letters, it read "DAN THE MAN!" Below the picture, it read "Student Council Elections, September 21. Vote Dan The Man!" There was a glittery border around the edge of the poster, and a bunch of stars.

It looked like Madalaine had spent at least a couple hours working on it. And this was only one of her three posters.

"Let me see the other ones," I said.

Madalaine unrolled the other two posters. They were almost the same as the first one, they just each used a different color for the glitter and bubble letters. The first one was red. The second one was blue. The third one was green.

"Do you think he'll like them?" Madalaine asked anxiously. "He hasn't seen them yet. I was thinking about maybe just putting them up without telling him. Then he'll be surprised when he sees them. And really happy."

I stared at the three posters, which were far better than the ones Daniel and I had made. Finally, I asked, "Where'd you get a picture?"

"On Instagram."

"Daniel has an Instagram?" This was news to me. I knew what Instagram was because Lacey had one. Lacey also had a Facebook page, a Twitter account, a YouTube channel, a cell phone, and her own laptop. Daniel and I didn't have any of those things yet. At least, I hadn't thought Daniel had any of those things.

"I know, right?" said Madalaine. "I was surprised too, because he'd never mentioned it before. But he started following me last night, and I was like, 'oh, this is perfect. I can just print out one of his pictures from

Instagram and use it for the poster!'"

Why hadn't Daniel told me he'd gotten an Instagram account? When did he create it? Why hadn't I known about it?

I looked again at the posters. Aside from the fact that Madalaine had clearly worked on them for hours, there was something else I didn't like about them. "His name is *Daniel*. He goes by *Daniel*. Not *Dan*. Nobody ever calls him Dan."

"Some people do," said Madalaine. "In some of our classes. But yeah, I know he mainly goes by Daniel. It's not catchy enough, though. I figured 'Dan the Man' would be a good slogan. I couldn't think of anything that rhymed with Daniel."

"But he's not even a man. He's twelve," I said.

Madalaine rolled her eyes and laughed. "No duh. It's just a slogan. It's just basically saying that Daniel is *the* guy. You know, *the* one people want to vote for for student council."

"Hm."

A slightly worried look passed Madalaine's face. "What? You don't think he'll like it? Was it a little over-the-top? Maybe I shouldn't have made posters. I just felt so bad…"

I dearly wanted to tell Madalaine that yes, it was over-the-top for her to make posters for Daniel, especially since she was supposedly competing against him for a spot on student council, and that Daniel would be mad at her for taking a photo from his Instagram account without asking him, and that he wouldn't like the slogan. But in all honesty, he probably wouldn't be mad about the picture, and he probably wouldn't have a problem with the slogan. And Madalaine was such a genuinely nice person that to tell her she shouldn't have made the posters in the first place would just be mean. So I said, "No, he'll probably like them. He'll be glad you made the posters. Really."

"You really think so? Oh, I hope so. I worked really hard on them. Where do you think I should put them up?"

I tried to think of some of the least conspicuous places in the school. "You know that hallway where all the Tech Ed classes are? You know the part that turns off and leads to the janitors' closet? That might be a good place. I don't think anyone else has posters up in that hallway yet, so your poster would be the only one anyone would see when they went down there."

Madalaine wrinkled her nose. "Yeah...but I think

there's a reason nobody else has posters down there. Nobody ever *goes* down there, except the janitors and maybe a couple kids who are up to no good. People need to *see* the posters. Ooh, I know where I'll put one. How about right in front of the doors leading out of the cafeteria, so it's the first thing people see when they leave from lunch?"

By the time we arrived at school, Madalaine had picked the three most conspicuous places in the building to place her posters.

We were heading off the bus and into the school when we heard someone yelling, "Madalaine!"

It was Daniel's voice. We both turned in his direction.

"Hey," Daniel ran toward us. "Look what my parents gave me last night," he said, thrusting something into Madalaine's hand. I stared. It was a cell phone.

Travis and Lacey had cell phones. They'd each gotten one for their thirteenth birthday. I'd assumed Daniel and I would each be getting one for our thirteenth birthdays as well. But Daniel wasn't thirteen yet. He wouldn't be thirteen until February. What was up with his parents deciding to give him a phone five whole months in advance? And why hadn't my parents been in on the deal and given me one too?

"Yay!" Madalaine was excited. "You finally got a phone! Can I give you my number?"

"Sure. And then I'll send you a text, so you can have my number too."

"Awesome!"

I all the sudden felt very left out and very, very young. Daniel now had a phone and an Instagram account. I had nothing.

"You didn't tell me you got a cell phone," I said accusingly.

"I just got it last night," said Daniel. "It was a total surprise. My mom said she and my dad had been talking, and they'd decided that now that I was in junior high I was ready for a phone. Especially since I'm doing programming club and hopefully student council. I might need to ask my parents to pick me up early or late or something."

"You could've shown me at the bus stop." I thought back to when we were on the bus, when Daniel had been showing Hunter something. It had most likely been his new phone. Had Daniel *wanted* to leave me out? Had he wanted to show all his other friends before he showed me?

"We didn't have a lot of time at the bus stop," said Daniel. "And I didn't want you to tell Madalaine, because I wanted to show it to her in person."

"I wouldn't have told Madalaine if you'd asked me not to tell her."

I don't even think Daniel heard me. He was busy looking at the rolled-up posters in Madalaine's arms. "What are those?"

"Um…" Madalaine glanced at me, and for a moment I felt included again. "A surprise."

"Yeah, top secret," I said, helping her out.

Daniel tried to grab one of the posters, but Madalaine slapped his hand away, laughing. "Hey! You'll find out later. I promise. Later today."

"In one of our classes?"

"I don't know exactly when."

"I think I already know what it is."

"Oh yeah? What's that?"

"Posters telling people to vote for you for student council."

"Maybe." Madalaine raised her eyebrows and grinned. "As I said, you'll find out later."

Daniel laughed and gave Madalaine a gentle push. I felt excluded again. Even though all they were doing was talking about what was on Madalaine's posters, they seemed like they were having such a good time.

The school day dragged for me. When it was finally lunch time, I went to my usual table to sit with Daniel, Madalaine, and the rest of their friends. But there was already someone in my seat.

"Excuse me," I said uncertainly.

The person in my seat turned around, and I recognized him. He was one of the kids who'd been with Daniel the day Daniel had yelled at me and said we were just neighbors. The one who'd made fun of me and called me a stalker.

He recognized me too. I could tell, because he got a leering sort of grin on his face. "Well, well, well! Looks like stalker girl has shown up. Looking for your 'boyfriend'?"

"He's not my boyfriend. He's my friend."

"Ohhhhh, really? *Just* your friend? But you're going to be boyfriend and girlfriend *eventually*, right?"

"Hey Tyler, shut up and leave her alone," said Daniel.

Tyler laughed. "Defending the future girlfriend. Nice move."

"She's not my future girlfriend. I told you, she's just

my neighbor. But she does usually sit with us."

"And you're in her seat," Madalaine added.

"What? I gotta give up my seat to stalker girl?"

"Her name is Alanna," said Madalaine. I could tell she didn't like Tyler.

"Her name is a llama?"

"*Alanna*," I said. The fact that my name sounded like *a llama* had been cool when I was in kindergarten, but it had gotten old fast. Especially when jerks like Tyler always had to make comments about it. "And you're in my seat."

"Give her her seat," said Madalaine.

Tyler made a big show of rolling his eyes and huffing as he stood up and left the seat open for me. "Fine. I was done anyway."

I sat down. Madalaine, across the table, leaned toward me. "Sorry about that. Most of us don't really like Tyler. He's just in our classes, and he hangs out with Ross and Hunter a little bit." Her face brightened. "Hey! Guess what! Daniel saw the posters! I put them up during homeroom."

"Your posters?" Daniel was suddenly in the conversation. He spoke to me: "Yeah, you know those rolled-up posters Madalaine had this morning on the bus? I thought they were posters for her campaign, but they were posters for *me*! And they're amazing! Much better than the ones we made. Have you seen them? She got my picture from Instagram! I didn't even think about putting a picture on the poster!" He grinned at Madalaine.

Madalaine seemed to blush a little. "I'm glad you like them."

"They're awesome! Now I feel like I should make some for you. Except mine wouldn't be that good, 'cause I'm not so good at art and stuff."

"It's fine," said Madalaine. "Don't worry about it. I have enough posters."

I was a little late to FCS that afternoon, because I'd stopped in the bathroom on the way. When I got to my table, Madalaine, Amanda, and Shelly were all giggling. "What's going on?" I asked.

"We're just talking about Daniel," said Shelly. "How he loved Madalaine's posters."

"I know, I'm so glad he did!" exclaimed Madalaine. "I hadn't been sure…"

I'd been sure. How could Daniel *not* like the posters? They were amazing. But I didn't like how excited Madalaine seemed about the fact that Daniel had liked her posters.

"Did you find out about basketball yet?" I asked
Amanda.

Amanda shook her head. "I keep forgetting to ask.
I'll ask tomorrow, I promise. Well, if I remember."

Mrs. Haller came around, passing out pieces of paper. I hoped they were recipes, and that we were finally
going to cook something. But they weren't. "Junior high
is when you first need to start thinking about what you
might want to do with your life once you graduate high
school," Mrs. Haller said. "You don't need to come to a
definite decision yet. But you do need to just get some
ideas in your mind about what interests you. On these
papers I'm passing out, I'd like you to brainstorm some
things you like to do."

Things I liked to do. The first thing I wrote was
Hang out with Daniel. I looked at it, then slowly crossed
out *Daniel* and wrote *friends.* I had other friends now. I
had Madalaine and Amanda and Shelly to hang out with
in FCS, and Travis to play basketball with. So Daniel
wasn't my *only* friend.

What else did I like to do? *Play basketball. Do art.
Play soccer. Listen to music. Rollerblade. Ride my bike. Play*

Wii. Go in Daniel's tree fort. Play in the backyard. Make weird desserts.

As I looked my list over again, I realized that if Daniel ever decided he didn't want to hang out with me at home anymore, I'd be in big, big trouble. Because aside from playing basketball, which was with Travis, and doing art and listening to music, which I could do by myself, every item on my list was something I did with Daniel.

Chapter 12

Time With Mom

When Daniel and I got off at our bus stop that day, Daniel had a weird sort of grin on his face. "What are you smirking about?" I asked.

"Who, me? I'm not smirking. What are you talking about?"

"You're smiling about something."

Daniel's grin grew even wider. "I just can't believe she made all those posters for me. That was really nice."

It was. It was *too* nice, and Daniel was *too* happy about it.

"She only did it because she felt bad that she signed up to run for student council after you'd told her you were going to," I told him.

"Still," said Daniel. "It was really nice. I wasn't expecting her to do that. I feel like I should do something back for her. But I don't know what."

He pulled his new phone out of his pocket and started staring down at the screen. I leaned over and watched him pull up his Contacts list, and tap Madalaine's name. It pulled up with her phone number, options to call or text her, and her picture. I could tell the picture had been taken in one of their classes together. "Nice picture," I said, mainly to see how Daniel would react.

"Yeah," he grinned. "I took it at the beginning of science when the teacher wasn't looking." He tapped the option to text and I watched what he typed out. *Thanx again for the posters. They're great! C u tomorrow.*

To my surprise, he handed the phone to me. "Do you think this is okay to send?" he asked. "I mean, I already thanked her for them at school. I don't want to go, you know, overboard."

I read the message over and over. "You spelled *thanks* wrong," I said.

"Yeah, I know. I did it that way on purpose. That's how people text. See? I spelled *see* and *you* wrong too. It just makes it shorter."

"Yeah, and people used to try to make things shorter when they had those old phones that didn't even have a full keyboard. Because they didn't want to spend all that time typing on the number keys. You have a smartphone. It would take about a quarter of a second to type two extra letters."

Daniel shrugged. "It's fine. You think the message is all right, though?"

I couldn't find anything else wrong with it, so I grudgingly handed the phone back to him. "Yeah. It's all right. What do you want to do when we get home?"

"Uhh…" said Daniel. "Actually, Hunter wanted me to Skype him at four. We're doing a project together for music, and we wanted to make sure we were both on the same page."

"Oh." I felt like a deflated balloon. I was getting that feeling more and more often around Daniel. "So, how long will that take?"

"Probably at least an hour?" Daniel did at least look apologetic. "And then my parents will be getting home, and we'll probably be having dinner, so…"

"So we're not going to hang out today."

"Right."

I hesitated, then asked, "Is Travis home?" Maybe he and I could play basketball together.

Daniel shrugged. "I don't know. We can check."

We went to Daniel's house and stepped inside. "Travis?" Daniel called. There was no answer. "Guess not," said Daniel.

"So he must be at my house!" *Finally,* I thought. *With Lacey, where he belongs.*

"Okay. Well… I guess you can go over and see if Travis and Lacey want to do something. I'm going to get ready to Skype Hunter."

I left Daniel's house and went across the lawn to my own. It was only once I reached the door that I realized I had no idea what I was going to do if Travis and Lacey were already hanging out together. It was fine when it was all four of us, or when there were just two of us. But Travis and Lacey and me, with no Daniel, would make me the odd one out.

I went inside anyway. The house was quiet, almost as quiet as Daniel's. Mom was in the living room, folding clothes. "Hi Mom. Are Lacey and Travis upstairs?"

"Lacey is," Mom answered, after giving me a hello hug. "I don't think Travis is here. How was your day at school?"

"He has to be here," I protested, ignoring her question. "He isn't at his house."

"Well, maybe he has some sort of after-school activity, or went over to a different friend's house. I know Lacey came in alone after school, and nobody else has come in since then other than you."

So I'd been wrong. Travis and Lacey weren't hanging out together, the way they should have been. I frowned.

"Honey, what's going on lately? You don't seem… yourself."

Too much. Too much was going on, and too much was changing.

"What's Daniel up to today?"

"Skyping his friend."

"Ah," I saw Mom make the connection. "Daniel's been spending less time with you, is that it?"

To my embarrassment, I felt tears come to my eyes.

"Oh honey…" Mom sat down on the couch and I cuddled up next to her. "You're at a tough age," she said, hugging me. "A new school, lots of new people in your life, all the sudden nothing's the same as it used to be…"

I managed to speak. "Yeah. And now Daniel's in programming club and he wants to be on student council and he's making all these other friends and it seems like he doesn't have time for me anymore. He said we could still be friends at home but now he wants to spend even his home time doing stuff with his other friends."

"I'm sorry," said Mom. "Growing up's really tough sometimes."

We sat there quietly together for a little bit. Then Mom asked, "Have you made any other friends? Or are there any people in your classes who you might want to get to know better?"

"A few girls in my FCS class," I sniffled. "But one of them is friends with Daniel too."

"Well, that's a good thing, isn't it?" Mom sounded confused. "If she's friends with Daniel and you're friends with Daniel, maybe the three of you could hang out to-gether."

"It doesn't really work that way," I whispered. "At lunch they always talk together and forget about me." It sounded awful, just saying it bluntly like that. But it was true.

As we continued to sit on the couch together, me lying against Mom with her arm around me, a glimmer of hope came to my mind. A way that I could become a little more included.

"Mom?" I asked, sitting up. "Could you get me a phone?"

"A phone? You mean like a cell phone?"

I nodded. "Daniel got one. He also got an Instagram account. Can I get a phone and an Instagram?"

"I'm not sure you really need a phone right now," said Mom. "We got one for Lacey in seventh grade because she was involved in a lot of activities. But you're not involved in any after-school activities, so I don't think you need a cell phone."

"How about an Instagram? Can I at least get an Instagram?"

"I don't know nearly enough about Instagram to tell you yes or no right now."

"Lacey has an Instagram." *And a Facebook, and a Twitter, and her own YouTube channel where she posts boring videos of herself reading essays she's written.* "Ask her about it."

"Maybe," said Mom. "We'll see."

And since it wasn't a flat-out no, the possibility that I might be able to get an Instagram account remained a small glimmer of hope on my horizon.

Chapter 13

Elections

By Friday the glimmer of hope was gone. Poof. Popped, like my balloon.

It had been a bad week. I'd had fun playing basketball with Travis on Tuesday—just on Tuesday, not Thursday, because he'd had a dentist appointment on Thursday—and Daniel and I had spent about thirty minutes together on Wednesday, trying to decide what to do, before Daniel got a call from Madalaine and decided to talk with her for fifty million hours. And you'd think, since Madalaine was my friend too, that Daniel would have said, "Hey, Alanna's here too, let me put you on speakerphone so all three of us can talk together!"

Not like it would have made much of a difference, since I probably wouldn't have had much of a chance to speak, but still, he could have offered. And he hadn't.

And now it was Friday. Student council voting day. Voting would be at lunch.

"Oh my gosh, I can't even think straight," said Madalaine on the bus ride to school. "The elections are today. And at the end of seventh period, we'll find out who's on student council!"

"How many people are running?" I asked.

"At least eight. And there are only five slots available. Oh, I really, really, *really* hope Daniel and I both make it! I was praying about it, like, *all* last night. You're voting, right?"

I nodded. I knew I would be voting. I just didn't know who I'd be voting for.

"How many people are we allowed to vote for?" I asked.

"Up to five. But you don't have to vote for that many. You could just vote for one or two or three or four people if you want."

I kind of wished you could only vote for one person. Then I'd just vote for Madalaine and that would be that.

The day passed pretty quickly for me until lunch.

For Madalaine, it probably crawled by. For Daniel too, most likely, except I wouldn't know because I hadn't talked to him at all except for a quick "Hi" at the bus stop.

The voting tables were set up right as you entered the lunchroom. All the current student council members (eighth graders) were sitting behind the booth, waving at everyone coming into the lunchroom. "Come vote for your new student council members!" they called.

I went over to the table. "Are you here to vote?" a girl asked me.

I nodded. She handed me a ballot. "You can vote for up to five people," she told me. "Just place a checkmark in the box next to the names of the people you want to vote for."

I looked at the ballot. Daniel and Madalaine were on the list, as well as Hunter, a boy from our lunch table named Max, and a girl from my classes named Ellen. Then there were three kids I didn't know.

I could vote for up to five people. It would be easy to vote for the five I knew, and leave blank the three I didn't know.

I put a checkmark next to Madalaine's name. Then I put one next to Hunter's. Then one next to Max's, and one next to Ellen's.

I could vote for one more person if I wanted.

My pencil hovered over Daniel's name. Student council was something he really wanted. And he was my best friend, and best friends are supposed to be supportive of what each other want. But if Daniel got on student council, that would be more time spent with his other friends, and less time spent with me. A *lot* less time spent with me.

I placed a checkmark next to the name of one of the kids I didn't know and stuffed my ballot in the ballot box before I could change my mind.

Then I walked over to the usual lunch table and acted like everything was perfectly normal. Madalaine and Daniel were arm-wrestling when I got there, and everyone was watching them, so I was able to slip into my normal seat without being noticed. Then Madalaine won the contest and everyone cheered and teased Daniel about being beat by a girl.

Madalaine looked up and saw me. "Hey! Alanna, did you vote?"

"Yep," I said.

"Did you vote for me?" Max asked.

"Or me?" asked Hunter.

"I voted for both of you. I voted for five people in all." It was safe to tell them that. Everyone would assume that Daniel was one of the other three.

"All right!" Hunter high-fived Max, who high-fived Daniel. I felt a little bad about not casting a vote for Daniel. But then again, it wasn't like anybody would ever know. When the votes came in at the end of the day, Daniel would either be one of the winners or one of the losers, and he wouldn't know the difference whether I voted for him or not.

The last three periods of the day dragged on for me, probably because I was now waiting for something too. Close to the end of seventh period, I would find out whether Daniel had made student council or not. Whether he'd be able to keep spending the same amount of time with me or not.

In FCS, Mrs. Haller showed us how to sew a running stitch. It wasn't cooking, but I was glad we were finally getting into some hands-on stuff. I felt bad for Madalaine, though. She could barely concentrate. She kept looking up at the loudspeaker in the front of the classroom, waiting for the announcement we knew was coming.

It came with five minutes to the end of the day,

right as we were cleaning up from our sewing. "Good afternoon, the votes are in for today's student council election. We have five new seventh graders who will be joining student council. Their names are Aryana Bradbury, Madalaine Carson, Hunter Lessard, Daniel Malone, and Max Naughton. The first student council meeting will be next Monday, September 24, after school. Thank you, and congratulations to our new student council representatives!"

Madalaine jumped up and down and threw her arms around the people closest to her—Shelly and me. "I made it! And Daniel made it! Yay! I'm sooooo happy!"

"Congratulations," said Shelly.

"Yeah, that's awesome," said Amanda.

"It is," I agreed, trying to make my voice sound sincere. And, well, it really was great that Madalaine had gotten onto student council, and I really was happy for her. I tried to focus on those good points.

But it was pretty hard to focus on the good points once school got out and we all headed to our buses. Madalaine saw Daniel walking a little bit ahead of us, and she ran over and gave him a hug from behind. The same exact kind of hug I'd given him that day in the hallway.

But Daniel didn't react the same way he'd reacted with me. He didn't act embarrassed or yell at her or anything like that. I was close enough to see exactly what he did.

He turned around and saw that it was her. He smiled—not his normal Daniel smile that I used to see all the time, but a new kind of smile, one I'd just recently started seeing on his face whenever Madalaine was around. A kind of shy but super pleased smile. His face looked a little pink, but not red like when I'd hugged him. And I had a feeling that it wasn't for the same reason either.

"Daniel!" Madalaine exclaimed ecstatically. "We made it! We both made it!"

"I know! It's awesome!" Daniel exclaimed, just as ecstatically.

And then, instead of getting mad at her for hugging him in front of his friends—because he *was* with Hunter and a few other kids, just like he'd been that day that I hugged him—he just kept looking at her and grinning.

And then he hugged her back.

Chapter 14

A Bike Ride

I knew that Daniel's schedule was about to get busy—even busier than it had been before he'd gotten elected to student council. So I made sure to get up early on Saturday and go over to his house, to claim him before someone called him or texted him or Skyped him or anything. It was a beautiful day, and I had a great idea that would involve all four of us—me, Daniel, Travis, and Lacey.

Since it was a weekend, Daniel's parents were home. And since they were home, the front door was unlocked, like it had always been all the years leading up to this one. As I opened the front door to stick my head in and call, "Helloooooooo!" I almost felt like I'd gone back in time, like things were the same as they'd always been before we'd started junior high.

Then Mr. Malone came to the door. "Alanna!" he exclaimed, giving me a hug. "Nice to see you! It's been a while."

I nodded. "Can I go in and see Daniel?"

"Well, I'm pretty sure they're still sleeping right now, since they had a pretty late night. But let's go check."

When he said 'they're', I assumed he meant Daniel and Travis. But as we walked through the kitchen, I saw that Travis was eating breakfast. He waved to me and I waved back to him. And then Mr. Malone said the thing that didn't make sense. "Are they still sleeping?"

"Think so," said Travis.

"Who?" I asked.

"Daniel and his friends."

I froze. "His friends are here?"

Mr. Malone looked at me, puzzled. "Yes. Hunter and Max. They slept over last night. I thought you knew that."

I hadn't known that. Hunter and Max had both gotten off at our bus stop the day before, but I'd assumed they were just going to hang out at Daniel's house for an hour or so before going home. Daniel had had a whole entire *sleepover* and hadn't mentioned it to me?

"Oh," I said. "Well, Daniel didn't tell me that, but...okay. Okay."

When we were younger—meaning, all the way up until the start of seventh grade—Daniel, Lacey, Travis and I used to have sleepovers together all the time. We'd all go to one of our two houses and stay up super late and eat a bunch of junk food and watch movies at 2am. I'd never been to a sleepover with anyone but those three. And, up until now, Daniel had never been to a sleepover other than with us three.

And now, once again, he was doing something new without me.

My idea for the four of us had been a bike ride. I pictured asking Daniel, Hunter, and Max if they all wanted to go on a bike ride with me. It could definitely work, if I invited Hunter and Max rather than Travis and Lacey. One of them could ride Travis's bike, and one could ride Lacey's. Maybe it would be fun.

But maybe Hunter and Max wouldn't want to go on a bike ride with me. They didn't know me very well, and they'd come to spend time with *Daniel*, not with me. Maybe even Daniel wouldn't want me along.

"Travis," I found myself saying. "Do you want to go on a bike ride with me and Lacey?" Taking a bike ride with Travis and Lacey would still leave me as the odd-ball, but it would be a more *comfortable* oddball-ness than going with Daniel and his friends. At least I'd known Travis and Lacey forever, and they'd known me forever, and I wouldn't feel like as *much* of an oddball or have to worry about how I was acting.

"Sure," said Travis. "When're you guys going?"

I shrugged. "When you finish breakfast. And whenever Lacey's ready. I haven't asked her yet." Lacey hadn't even known about the bike ride. I'd decided to invite Daniel and Travis first.

Travis took one last bite of cereal and put his bowl in the sink. "I'm done."

Travis said bye to his dad, and then he and I walked together over to my house. "Is that Daniel's *first* sleepover with Hunter and Max?" I asked, just to be sure.

"Yeah." Travis looked at me, a little concerned. "I didn't know he hadn't told you about it."

"It's okay," I said, even though it wasn't.

We walked into my house and I called out Lacey's name. "In my room," she called back.

"Come on," I grabbed Travis's arm and ran up the stairs. Lacey was on her computer, with her earbuds plugged in and a textbook spread out next to her. She looked surprised to see Travis with me.

"What are you doing, *homework* again?" I asked.

"I'm in an AP class," she told me. "And a bunch of honors classes. And it's high school. We get lots of homework."

"Well, Travis and I are going on a bike ride," I said. "You wanna come?"

Lacey looked at Travis and I could've sworn some sort of look passed between them. I didn't know how to read the look, or what it meant. I only knew that they had definitely exchanged some sort of look.

"Thanks for inviting me," said Lacey. "But I really need to get this essay done."

I rolled my eyes. "Come on. It's *Saturday*. You spend every single weekday working on homework. You need some fresh air and exercise!"

Lacey laughed. "You sound like Mom. No, really, this essay is due on Monday, and it's a big part of my grade. You guys go without me."

I tried to share an exasperated look with Travis. But he was just nodding. "All right, well, good luck on your essay," he said to Lacey.

"Thanks. Have fun on your bike ride."

As Travis and I left Lacey's room, I realized what the look they'd exchanged must have meant. Travis hadn't tried all that hard to get Lacey to come, and he hadn't seemed that disappointed when she said she had to do her homework. So that must have meant he hadn't really *wanted* her to come in the first place.

"Did you and Lacey have a fight?" I asked as I put my helmet on. I mounted my bike and pedaled over with Travis, back to his house so he could get his bike.

"No," he said, giving me a sort of weird look. "Why?"

I shrugged. "Just sorta seemed like it. Like you guys didn't want to be around each other."

Travis shook his head. "It wasn't that, it was...something else. It...she really does get a lot of homework. And she really does need to get it done. Believe me, I've seen her textbooks. They're huge. Much bigger than mine, since I'm just a dummy taking regular classes."

"You're not dumb," I said automatically, before realizing that he was trying to distract me from the real issue. "And you're acting really suspicious, and I still think you and Lacey had some sort of fight."

"We didn't have a fight," Travis said, swinging his leg over his bike seat to get on. "Now, where are we going?"

I hadn't really had anywhere planned. "Just around the neighborhood," I said. "And maybe that little path in the woods." A few streets down from where we lived, there was a little dirt trail that led to a small clearing with a couple picnic tables. "Actually, you wanna have a picnic?"

"A picnic? Sure!"

We went back into the Malones' house to get food. Mr. Malone was now in the living room, watching TV. "Back already?" he said when he saw us. "That was a short bike ride."

We both laughed. "Very short," said Travis. "No, we actually just came to get stuff for a picnic."

Travis and I were rummaging around in the cabinets and fridge when I heard voices. A moment later, Daniel, Hunter, and Max came into the kitchen. Hunter and Max froze when they saw me.

"Well, this is awkward, considering I'm in my boxers," said Hunter. "I didn't know you were going to be here."

I hadn't even noticed he was in his boxers until he brought it to my attention. I couldn't think of anything to say, so I just shrugged.

"I kind of see what Tyler means about you stalking Dan," said Max. "What are you doing here so early in the morning?"

He was full of it. It wasn't even early. I looked at Daniel, who was busy looking down at his feet and not standing up for me. *Fine*, I thought. *I'll stand up for myself then.* "Believe it or not," I said, grabbing a bag of Cheetos, "I'm not even here to hang out with Daniel. I know you guys are doing your own thing, and I'm cool with that. I'm here to hang out with one of my other friends. And we were actually just leaving. Come on, Travis."

We didn't talk again until we were both on our bikes and had started down the street. Then Travis said, "What's the deal between you and those guys?"

"Who, Hunter and Max? They don't like me." It wasn't exactly true. I ate at their table every day for lunch, and neither one of them had ever seemed to have a problem with it. But they'd certainly acted like they didn't like me, or at least didn't want me around, back at the Malones' house.

"Why not? How the heck could they not like you?"

I smiled a little at the question. Travis, at least, still thought I was worthy to hang out with. He didn't seem to think anything was embarrassing or shameful about me.

"Well, I'm not sure if they don't *like* me exactly, but they don't like it when I try to hang out with Daniel. They want him all to themselves."

"And you don't?"

I looked over and saw that Travis was smiling, as if he already knew my answer. And of course he did already know my answer. Yes, I did want Daniel all to myself. Maybe that was part of the problem.

"I just want things the way they used to be," I said. "You and Lacey and me and Daniel, hanging out every day, and I never had to worry about whether Daniel would *want* to hang out with me or not, because he always did, and Lacey didn't always have fifty million pounds of homework to do, and... yeah. Everything was different."

"It was," Travis agreed.

We reached a downhill section of the road then, and

both put on a burst of speed. We didn't talk again until we'd reached the trail into the woods.

"Do you wanna go first, or do you want me to go first?" Travis asked. The trail was only big enough for one bike at a time.

"I don't care," I said.

"I'll go first," Travis decided, and pedaled on ahead. I followed him down the bumpy dirt path, punctuated with gnarled roots and random rocks. A few times I almost wiped out, but I managed to stay on. Finally, we reached the picnic area and got off our bikes.

"And now," said Travis with a flourish, pulling off his backpack and unzipping it to get the food. "Time for lunch."

I laughed. "Didn't you just have breakfast right before we left?"

"What, you think I should call this my 'breakfast number two' rather than my lunch?"

I nodded, satisfied with his response. "That way we can both be eating breakfast at the same time. I didn't eat anything before I came over."

"You knew you were going on a bike ride, and you didn't *eat* anything beforehand? Alanna, you're a little crazy, you know that?"

119

"Yep, I know." Somehow there was a difference between Travis calling me crazy and Daniel's friends thinking I was crazy. Travis meant it in a nice way.

We sat down at the picnic table and Travis handed me the bag of Cheetos and an apple. For himself, he took out a bag of Doritos and another apple.

"Let's have a toast," I said, suddenly feeling in a silly mood. "To..." I looked around. "To bike riding!"

"To bike riding!" Travis and I held up our apples and clinked them against each other. "And may we have many more excellent bike rides in the future," he added in a funny accent, and I laughed.

And for a moment—even though everything was different from how it used to be—my world felt perfect again.

Chapter 15

Betrayed

Monday felt weird to begin with. Daniel and I didn't talk much at the bus stop, and then when the bus came, he went to sit with his friends and I saw them looking over at me and whispering. Probably talking about how I was a stalker or something like that. I sat next to Madalaine, and she asked me how my weekend was and we talked until we got to school. Nothing out of the ordinary about that. Still, something felt off. Maybe somehow, in the back of my mind, I knew what was going to happen at lunch. There was no possible way I could have known—okay, aside from the clues I'd been seeing all along that I hadn't wanted to pick up on—but somehow, I must have known, just a little.

Amanda found me next to my locker after second period. "Oh my gosh, I'm so glad I found you!" She was out of breath and panting.

"What's going on?" I asked.

"Basketball tryouts. I just found out on Friday, but then I forgot to tell you in class, so I had to find you as soon as I could. They're today."

I stared at her. "*Today?*"

"Yeah. Right after school. In the gym. Well, obviously in the gym. Anyway, yeah. I'm so sorry I didn't tell you on Friday, I totally spaced it."

It was Monday. And it was the day of Daniel's first student council meeting, which meant that I wouldn't have to worry about missing out on time with him if I went to tryouts. Of course, I'd probably have to worry about missing time with him if I made the team.

"When does the team meet?" I asked.

Amanda shrugged. "I heard they meet a couple times a week, but I don't know exactly when. They'll probably give us more information once we're actually on the team. Like a schedule and everything. The season hasn't officially started yet."

The thought that the basketball season might interfere with the very tiny amount of time I had left with Daniel made me hesitant. "Maybe I shouldn't try out."

"What are you talking about? Of course you're trying out! I need a friend to try out with me. I'd be too nervous otherwise. Come on!"

The fact that Amanda considered me her friend made me happy. "Okay," I said. "I'll try out, but I might not join the team. Just so you know."

Amanda didn't press me as to why. She just held up her hand for a high five. I slapped it. "Hey Amanda?"

"Yeah?"

"I'm the only seventh grader in the entire school who doesn't yet have a cell phone. Can I use yours to call my mom and let her know I'll be home late?"

"Sure," Amanda laughed and pulled her phone out of her pocket. "And you're not the only seventh grader without a phone; there's this girl in my classes who's always complaining about not having one. She's super annoying."

"Great. Just what I wanted. To have a similarity with some super annoying girl!" Amanda and I both laughed. I was surprised at how easy it was to talk to her. Was this what it was like, having a friend other than Daniel, Travis, Lacey, and Madalaine?

"Here you go," said Amanda, handing me the phone. "Pretend you're still looking in your locker for something. I'll hide you."

I took the phone, and Amanda stepped in front of me so I was hidden between her and the locker. We technically weren't allowed to use cell phones in school, so it was nice that she was hiding me and keeping a lookout for teachers. I called my mom's cell phone, but since she was at work, it went right to voicemail. "Hi Mom," I said quietly. "Um, yeah, this is Alanna. I had to use my friend Amanda's phone because I don't have my own phone. But I might need a phone soon because I'm trying out for the basketball team. Today. That's why I'm calling. I'll be coming home on the late bus, so…yeah. That's all. Love you."

I called my dad as well, and left about the same message on his voicemail. Halfway through me leaving the message, the bell rang. I hurried up and finished the message, then gave the phone back to Amanda. "Thanks."

"No problem. See you at tryouts!" We both raced off to our classes.

Maybe the reason the awful news came as such a surprise was because I was in such a good mood for the first half of the day.

At lunchtime, I went to my usual table with Daniel and Madalaine and their friends from their classes. Madalaine seemed super giggly and even happier than usual, but I didn't pay much attention at first.

That is, until Madalaine started snitching fries from Daniel's plate. "Hey," I said to her, because Daniel doesn't like it when people take his food—I know because I used to do it all the time back in second grade before he got even with me by dumping my chocolate milk all over my lunch. "Eat your own food."

Madalaine just giggled and put her finger to her lips.

"He's gonna get mad," I warned her.

Just then Daniel noticed Madalaine's hand creeping over to his tray to grab a fry. "Hey!" he exclaimed, slapping her hand away.

Madalaine burst into laughter. "Is this really the first time you noticed? I've been stealing stuff from you since you sat down!"

"Oh yeah? Well, thanks for confessing, robber. You're gonna pay for it now!" His face didn't match his words. He was grinning as he leaned over and started tickling Madalaine, who hunched over and started laughing hysterically.

Kiara, one of Daniel and Madalaine's friends from their classes, was sitting next to me, across the table from Daniel and Madalaine. "You guys make the cutest couple," she commented.

I'd just taken a sip of milk and almost spit it back into the carton. "They're not a couple," I told Kiara. "They're just friends."

"Nuh-uh, haven't you heard? Hey, you guys are a couple now, right? Dan? Maddie?"

"What? Daniel, *stop*, Kiara's talking to me!" Madalaine was still laughing as she straightened up and faced Kiara. Daniel gave her one last flick on the arm, which she returned, and then they both gave Kiara their attention, grinning and pink-faced.

"You guys are a couple now, right?" Kiara repeated.

Madalaine grinned at Daniel, and for the first time since I'd met her, her smile looked a bit shy. "Yes," she answered. "He asked me in first period. We're official."

The world was suddenly swirling around me and I wondered if I was going to pass out. What? Daniel and Madalaine were a couple? Since when? Since first period. But—but—they couldn't be. How *could* they? Daniel was *mine*. Everybody knew that, didn't they? Okay, maybe not *everyone*. Maybe not Kiara and Hunter and Max and Tyler and all of Daniel and Madalaine's other friends that they'd just met this year.

But Daniel knew that.

And Madalaine knew that.

And both of them had just betrayed me.

Chapter 16

Tryouts

I couldn't stay in the lunchroom. I couldn't stay there while my not-friends sat across from me all grinny and giggly and happy about the fact that they were now a couple, and everyone around them cheered them on and gave congratulations. I got up, taking my lunch tray with me, and started walking away.

"Alanna! Where are you going?" Madalaine called out.

I don't remember what I said to her. I might have said the bathroom or I might have mumbled something unintelligible or I might have said nothing at all. All I knew was that I needed to get away from her. How *could* she betray me like that? We'd made a pact!

I went to the bathroom and spent the rest of lunch in there. I couldn't go back out and face Madalaine and Daniel. I didn't even know how I was going to face Madalaine in seventh period. That pact we'd made at the beginning of the year with Shelly and Amanda—the one that none of us would go after a boy that any of the rest of us liked—did that mean *nothing* to her all the sudden?

And Daniel! Okay, so he'd been messing things up for a while now, joining activities without me, telling me not to hang around with him at school, spending less and less time with me. But I could deal with all that, as long as I had the assurance that Daniel and I would still be best friends and that someday we'd start dating and then eventually get married once we were all grown up.

Now everything I'd always known about my future was up in the air.

The bell rang and I didn't want to go to fifth period. But I knew I'd just get in trouble if I skipped, and besides, neither Daniel nor Madalaine was in my fifth period class. Because they were in all their classes *together.*

Fifth and sixth period went way too quickly. Pretty soon it was time for FCS.

I walked slowly toward the FCS classroom. Usually this was my favorite class, because I got to talk with my friends. But starting today, I'd be talking with my two friends and my *not*-friend.

The bell had just rung when I reached the classroom. I slowly stepped in and went over to our table, where Amanda, Shelly, and my not-friend sat. All three of them were giggling. "Hi," I said to Amanda and Shelly, purposely not looking at Madalaine.

"Hi," said Amanda. "Did you hear the news?"

"What news?"

"Madalaine's news!"

I had a pretty good idea what that news was. "Yeah. I heard it," I said flatly.

"About her and Dan Malone dating? Isn't that the cutest thing you've ever heard? They're both on student council, and they're in, like, all their classes together, and she's had a crush on him since, like, the beginning of the school year. She just told us."

She never told me. All the similarities Amanda had just listed off—I had more. I'd lived next door to Daniel all my life. I'd gone to the same elementary school as Daniel. Daniel and I had decided that we were a couple, practically, when we were five years old. Daniel and I had a million memories together and had known each other *forever*.

I wanted to bring up the pact. I wanted to remind them all—especially Madalaine—what we'd all agreed upon way back at the beginning of the year. *We won't get jealous of each other and we won't hold grudges. And we won't start hating each other's guts if we all fall for the same boy.* Okay, maybe I was breaking the pact a little too, because I sure felt like I hated Madalaine's guts right then. But only because she had broken the pact first. In fact, if I remembered correctly, she'd broken the part that *she* had made up! *We won't go out with a boy who any of the others of us already have dibs on.*

I had just opened my mouth to say something about the pact when Mrs. Haller began speaking. "All right, ladies and gentlemen, we're going to get right to work today," she said. "Grab your sewing projects and get started, and raise your hand if you need any help!"

"Madalaine, you should totally give your project to Daniel when you're done," said Amanda.

"Yeah!" exclaimed Shelly. "That would be so cute!"

Madalaine gave them both a look. "Guys, it's a little stuffed pillow made out of *flowery* fabric. I don't think he'll be interested."

"He might if it came from you," Amanda pointed out.

My not-friend looked at me. "What do you think, Alanna? You know him best. Would he appreciate it, or be like, 'Um…'?"

"He'd probably say, 'What's this crap? I don't want it,'" I said. Madalaine, Shelly, and Amanda all stared at me.

"You really think he'd say that? To *Madalaine*?" asked Shelly.

Of course I didn't. Daniel wasn't rude like that. Even if he got a gift he didn't like from someone other than Madalaine, he wouldn't say something like that. And if he got a gift he didn't like from Madalaine, he'd still probably be all over it like it was the best thing he'd ever seen. But my friends and my not-friend didn't need to know that. Madalaine was right. I did know him best. That meant I had all the power.

"Yep," I said. "And he wouldn't tell you, most likely, but he'd probably start thinking you were a little crazy in the head for giving him something like that. But go ahead, give it to him if you don't believe me."

I'd done my job. Madalaine looked unsure now.

"Alanna…" she said hesitantly. "Are you… do you have a problem with Daniel and me dating? Is that why you left the lunchroom early? You seem upset about something."

Did she really have to ask?

I was all set to say that yes, *of course* I had a problem with Madalaine and Daniel dating, and that I couldn't believe they would betray me like that. But I stopped myself. I wasn't sure I could trust myself not to start screaming right there in class.

"No," I lied. "I'm not upset. I just have a lot going on right now."

"Ohhh," Something like understanding came over Madalaine's face. "You have your basketball tryouts today, right? Is that what it is?"

I nodded, glad for the excuse. "Yeah. I'm just a little nervous. It's fine."

Mrs. Haller had a rule that we were allowed to listen to music—on phones, iPods, whatever—while we sewed, as long as we used headphones and didn't spend a bunch of time picking out what songs we wanted to listen to. For the first time since we'd started the sewing project, I was grateful for that rule. Even though I didn't have a phone or iPod of my own, my friends and not-friend all did, and Amanda and Shelly had already pulled theirs out and put their earbuds in.

"Can I share your earbuds?" I asked Shelly. I didn't even care what she was listening to.

Shelly nodded and passed one earbud to me. The song she was listening to was half rap, half country, with a little bit of disco thrown in, and it had a weird beat. But I didn't care. As long as I had an earbud in my ear, people would be less likely to talk to me.

It felt like forever before the bell finally rang for the end of school. Madalaine grinned. "See you guys later. Gotta go meet Dan for student council!"

"They are so adorable," said Shelly as Madalaine left. "Well, I gotta go catch my bus."

"And we have to get to basketball tryouts!" exclaimed Amanda, speaking for herself and me. "Bye Shelly."

Amanda and I headed to the gym together. "Are you ready for this?" she asked me.

I shrugged. "I guess so."

Amanda looked at me sideways. "Do you *want* to join the team? I feel kind of like I'm pushing you or something. If it's not something you want to do, don't do it."

I thought about it. My main hesitation for joining the team had been less time with Daniel. But now that Daniel had betrayed me...

Suddenly, I wanted more than anything to join the team. "Yes," I said definitively. "I want to join the team. I'm just a little nervous, that's all."

"You'll do fine," said Amanda. Then she paused. "I mean, I've never actually seen you play. So actually I have no idea how you'll do." She looked so confused I had to laugh. Then she started laughing too. "I'm sorry, that wasn't very encouraging."

"It's fine," Somehow laughing with Amanda, on top of realizing that I no longer needed to worry about basketball conflicting with my time with Daniel, had made all my doubts go away. I was more ready than ever to try out and make the team. "My friend Travis, Daniel's brother, he thinks I'm a good player. And he plays for his school, so he'd know."

"Oh. Okay then, as I said at first, you'll do fine. Just do your best."

We entered the locker room and Amanda changed into her gym clothes. I didn't have anything to change into, but I was wearing a T-shirt, jeans, and sneakers— nothing fancy—so Amanda said I'd be okay for tryouts.

When we got into the gym, Amanda found some friends from her core classes and started talking to them. She introduced me to them, but I immediately forgot all their names.

Eventually, a coach blew a whistle and told us all to go sit on the bleachers. "Here's how we're going to do it," he explained. "I'm going to run several different drills, which you'll all be part of. This includes layups, foul shots, passing drills, and dribbling drills. While you do the drills, my assistants and I will be watching your technique and assessing whether we think you'd be a better fit for the Level 1 team or the Level 2 team. Everyone here will make it onto one of the two teams. The Level 2 team is the more competitive of the two— that's the one that has away games against other schools. The Level 1 team is designed primarily to help you work on your skills and become a better player."

"Meaning, the Level 2 team is the *real* team and the Level 1 team is just the team they stuff everyone else on so they don't have to say anyone failed tryouts," Amanda whispered to me. I nodded.

"Of course, if you do make it on the Level 1 team after this tryout, don't worry, you still have a chance to move up to the Level 2 team. That will depend on your performance during Level 1 games."

"We better make it on the Level 2 team," I muttered to Amanda. "Level 1 sounds like just a practice league!"

"It is," said Amanda. She looked nervous.

The coach asked if anyone had questions, and a couple girls did, but not me or Amanda. Finally, we started the drills.

We did a passing drill first. We all lined up facing each other, and passed a ball back and forth down the line. Then we did another passing drill where two of us teamed up and passed the ball back and forth down the court before shooting it. Amanda and I were partners for that one, and we did well on it. Amanda even made the basket.

Then we did layups. I got to do five. I made one and missed the other four. Yikes.

Then it was my specialty. Foul shots. We each got to take five of those. I walked up confidently to the foul line and took a shot.

I missed.

I took my second shot.

I missed again.

What's wrong with me? I wondered. *I was making all the shots when I was playing with Travis.*

Oh. Maybe that was it. Basketball on a court was a lot different from basketball in a driveway. And taking shots with a whole bunch of people watching me was a lot different from taking shots with just one friend watching me.

I closed my eyes and pretended I was in Travis's driveway. Then I opened my eyes again and took note of where the basket was, how far away and at what angle. Then I closed my eyes again, and shot.

I made it!

I sunk my other two foul shots easily. Then we moved on to dribbling drills, in which I did fine. Then tryouts were over.

"You did great," Amanda told me as we went out into the hallway to get some water. "You'll definitely make the Level 2 team, no question."

"I'm sure you will too," I said truthfully. Amanda hadn't done as well as I had on the foul shots, but she'd made every single layup.

"We'll find out on Thursday."

"Yeah."

On Thursday we would find out which team we were on. And next week, practices would start. Coach hadn't given us an exact schedule yet, but he had said that each team met two to three times a week, sometimes combined and sometimes separate.

A day ago I would have been hoping my team would meet on Tuesdays and Thursdays, so I could still hang out with Daniel on Mondays, Wednesdays, and Fridays. But in light of what had happened earlier, I now was hoping for the reverse.

I hoped my team would meet on all the days Daniel didn't have after-school activities.

Chapter 17

Enemies

I had decided by the next morning that Madalaine was my number-one enemy, and Daniel was my number-two enemy. The reason Madalaine was my number-one was because her offense was worse than Daniel's. True, Daniel hadn't been a very good friend to me since we'd started junior high, and true, he had started dating someone else. But Madalaine had broken a *pact*. Particularly the part of the pact that *she* had suggested.

I purposely held off until almost the last minute before going to the bus stop. I was hoping the bus would already be there and I wouldn't have to stand there alone with Daniel. But I mistimed it. I wasn't as late as

I'd wanted to be.

"Hey," Daniel greeted me.

"Hey," I greeted him back, just as disinterestedly.

As the bus started rolling up our street, I realized something. I usually sat next to Madalaine on the bus! I'd have to spend an entire ride to school next to my number-one enemy!

"So," I heard myself saying to Daniel. "Since Madalaine's your girlfriend now, do you want to sit next to her on the bus?"

Daniel looked surprised. "You don't mind?"

I mind that she's your girlfriend. "Nope."

"Well… I mean, I usually sit next to Hunter, but maybe for today… I mean, do you think she'd want me to sit with her?"

Do you think she'd want me to sit with her? Really? What kind of question was that? "Yes, she'd want you to sit with her," I said, right as the bus pulled to a stop.

We got on and Daniel sat right down in my usual seat, next to Madalaine. Now I had nowhere to sit. I wasn't about to sit with Daniel's friends, who thought I was a stalker. I wished Amanda or Shelly took this bus.

"Alanna, where are you going to sit?" my number-one enemy asked me.

I shrugged, trying to pretend like I didn't care.

"Come squeeze in with us. Three of us can fit in one seat. Or we can kick Dan out if we don't all fit." Madalaine grinned.

I expected Daniel to correct her on his name. He'd never been Dan or Danny. Nobody had ever called him either of those names. From the time he was a baby, everyone had always called him Daniel.

But he didn't. "Hey!" he exclaimed, laughing. "Whatever. I mean, it's technically Alanna's seat anyway."

"Yeah, but it would be so much fun if it was all three of us," said Madalaine.

"Hey!" This time it was the bus driver. He was yelling at me. "Sit down! We need to get moving!"

Daniel scooched over, squishing Madalaine against the window. "Are you going to sit with us?" he asked. Madalaine giggled and her face turned pink, probably from being so close to Daniel.

I spied an empty seat a couple rows back. "No, I'll sit back there."

The ride to school was lonely. At the next stop, some random eighth grader came and sat next to me, but he had his headphones on and was playing games on his phone the entire time. I could see Madalaine and Daniel three rows in front of me, and they looked like they were having a grand old time. I couldn't hear what they were saying, but they were definitely laughing and enjoying being together.

I felt isolated. I reminded myself that I shouldn't care. Daniel and Madalaine were my enemies, after all, not my friends. They had betrayed me.

So why did I kind of wish I had chosen to sit with them?

They're not my friends, I reminded myself. *They don't really want me with them, and I don't really want to be with them.*

I didn't sit with them at lunch. Instead, I looked around to see if I could find Amanda. I finally located her, sitting with Shelly and some other girls several tables down from the table where my not-friends were sitting. Heart pounding, I walked in their direction. *What if they don't want me either?* I wondered.

But I didn't have to worry. Shelly saw me and waved, and that made it easier to come over. Then Amanda looked up and noticed me. "Alanna! Come sit with us!"

The girl next to Shelly moved over, and I sat down next to her. "This is Alanna," said Amanda to the table in general. "She's in FCS with me and Shelly."

"I remember you from basketball tryouts," said a girl with a long brown braid. "I'm Kaitlyn."

"Yeah, I was there too," said a blond girl with braces. "I'm Maggie."

The rest of the table went around introducing themselves. Then Maggie started talking about some boy she knew from her core classes, and it turned out this girl Jamie knew him too. But the rest of us didn't, and that was nice. Unlike Daniel and Madalaine's table, the girls at Shelly and Amanda's table weren't all from the same core class group. It was nice not being the *only* one out of the loop. I hoped Daniel and Madalaine could see me. I hoped they could see that I could have fun without them, and that I didn't need them. But more likely than not, they hadn't even noticed my absence.

Two periods later, I was on my way to FCS when I heard my name. "Alanna!"

I turned around to see who was calling me, then immediately pretended I hadn't noticed. It was Madalaine.

"Alanna!" She caught up with me. "Where were you

144

at lunch today?"

So she had noticed. "Sitting somewhere else," I said nonchalantly.

"Well, obviously, but *where?*"

"With Shelly and Amanda."

"Oh." Madalaine looked like she wanted to ask why, but she didn't. "Are you going to sit with us tomorrow?"

Was it just me, or did it seem like she really wanted me to?

I shrugged. "I don't know. Why?"

"'Cause we missed you, silly!" Madalaine smiled, but then her expression became serious. "No, seriously, if you want to sit with Shelly and Amanda during lunch, that's fine. You can sit wherever you want. I'm just saying that *I* like having you at *our* table. But it's your choice."

She continued walking, but I stood there. Madalaine was my enemy. Why did it still sort of feel like she was my friend?

Chapter 18

Talking With Lacey

I wanted to hate Madalaine for going out with Daniel. I really, *really* wanted to hate her.

But it was hard.

Madalaine was simply A Very Nice Person. She smiled and said hi to me every time she saw me. She acted like she actually *wanted* to be around me, unlike Daniel. And on Wednesday, she went out of her way to give me some Skittles on the bus. She was sitting with Daniel, and I was sitting a couple rows behind them, all alone, just like we'd been the previous morning. (The previous afternoon, Mom had picked me up for a doctor's appointment, so I hadn't had to worry about it.) I had already sat down when Madalaine took out the Skittles and started sharing them with Daniel, and then she turned around and held up the bag and asked, "Alanna? Do you want some?"

It's hard to hate someone like that.

Daniel and Madalaine had a student council meeting after school on Wednesday, so I rode the bus home alone. As in, even more alone than usual. When I got home, the house was quiet.

"Mom?" I called. "Lacey?"

"Upstairs," Lacey's voice called back.

I went up and found Lacey in her room, on—what a surprise—her computer. "Are you stuck to that thing?" I asked her.

"Stuck to what thing?" Lacey asked, her eyes never leaving the screen.

"Your computer."

"Basically." Lacey finally took her eyes off the screen and looked at me, smiling. "What's up?"

I was so surprised that she was actually paying more attention to me than to her computer, that I didn't answer right away. Then I realized that she really wanted to know.

I shrugged. "I guess I'm just bored."

"Where's Daniel?"

"Some student council meeting."

"Oh. Sweet."

"Yeah, sweet for him." I looked at my sister. There was no possible way she could understand where I was coming from. Lacey had been on student council in junior high. She'd been involved in practically every club and activity there was. If anyone could understand the way I was feeling, what with Daniel not having time for me anymore and choosing someone else over me, it would be Travis, not Lacey. I suddenly wondered if Travis had gone through anything similar when he and Lacey had entered junior high.

Well, even if he had experienced Lacey not spending as much time with him as before, he hadn't experienced the other part. The worse part. I knew for a fact that Lacey had never had a boyfriend.

Lacey was studying me closely. "Alanna... I know you miss spending all your time with Daniel. I understand that. But you guys are in junior high now, so it's okay for him to be kind of branching out and doing some things without you. You tried out for basketball, right?"

"Yeah."

"See? Once you start practices, you'll be having more fun, I promise. And you've made some other friends already, right? Those girls from your FCS class?"

I rolled my eyes. "Yeah, except one of them is now my *ex*-friend because she broke the pact we made together and started dating Daniel. So I've been trying to hate her, but she's a really hard person to hate."

Lacey looked like she was trying not to laugh. "Why is it necessary to hate her?"

Really? She had to ask? I had just explained everything to her. "Be*cause*," I said. "She's Daniel's *girlfriend*. And *I'm* supposed to be Daniel's girlfriend. And she *knew* that, and we made a pact at the beginning of the year that none of us would go out with a boy who we knew one of the others liked. *She* was the one who came up with that part of the pact. And she broke it."

"Hmm." Lacey frowned. "And why is it hard to hate her?"

"Because…" I tried to organize my thoughts. "Because she's my *friend*. At least, she was my friend. She was, like, the first person who was nice to me when I started junior high, and she always talks to me and

149

doesn't care if I'm a little… you know, random or whatever. She always says hi to me when she sees me and she always wants me to sit with her on the bus and at lunch and everything. And she shares Skittles with me for no reason."

"Hmm." Lacey was still thinking. "So is she, you know, fake-nice to you? Like she pretends to be all nice and sweet and innocent and then stabs you in the back? I hate people like that."

"No…" I hadn't known Madalaine for long, but I knew she wasn't like that. "She's genuine. I can tell she's genuine. I mean, she actually likes me and all that."

"Hmm," Lacey said a third time. "So she's genuine, and she actually likes you, but she also broke a pact you guys made? Something doesn't add up."

"Well…" I didn't want to believe that Madalaine wasn't actually genuine. And in all honesty, I didn't believe it. Madalaine *was* genuine. You could just tell. Madalaine really did like me. She really did consider me her friend.

Which meant… what?

"Alanna," said Lacey seriously. "Did you ever actually *tell* this girl that you liked Daniel? I mean, I didn't know you liked him —in *that* way— until just now.

Maybe she didn't know either."

"Of course she knew I liked Daniel!" Even as I said that, a little bit of uncertainty crept into my mind. Madalaine *did* know that, right? At least that I had dibs on him. Because I'd told her all about how Daniel and I were going to marry each other when we grew up, right?

Or... I tried to think back to those first few days of school, when Madalaine and Daniel were getting to know each other, and then when Madalaine and I were getting to know one another, and when Madalaine was asking me questions about Daniel... *Had* I ever said that Daniel and I were going to get married when we were older? Or had I just talked about what good friends we were then?

"So how long have you liked him?" asked Lacey.

I didn't know how to answer that question. It wasn't exactly a matter of how long I'd *liked* him; it was that I'd always known we were supposed to be together. We'd decided that when I was five. So I said, "Seven years?"

"You've had a crush on Daniel for *seven years*? Since kindergarten?" Lacey looked skeptical.

"Well, yeah. I mean, that's when we planned out our futures, remember? Me and Daniel, and you and Travis? We were in kindergarten, and you guys were in second grade."

Lacey put her head in her hands and heaved a huge sigh.

"Lacey? Is something wrong?"

"Alanna..." Lacey finally looked up. "Tell me honestly. Is that what this is all about? It's not so much that you *like* Daniel, it's just that you think you're *supposed* to like him because of some plans we made when you were in *kindergarten?*"

It sounded ridiculous, put like that. But that *wasn't* the reason I liked Daniel... right?

"Daniel's my best friend," I said hotly, even though he hadn't been treating me much like a best friend in the past couple weeks. "He's fun to hang out with, and he's funny, and he's nice, and he's good-looking, and I *do* like him. And I hate the fact that he's messing everything up."

"Things change," said Lacey. "That's life. Get used to it."

I scowled. Lacey was supposed to be on my side.

152

Lacey was supposed to understand, if not how I felt, at least that Daniel and I were supposed to be together. Just like she and Travis were supposed to be together. But come to think about it...

"I haven't seen you and Travis together a lot lately," I told her. "You guys are in high school now. Don't you think it's about time?"

"About time for what?"

"For you and Travis to start dating?"

Lacey put her hand over her face again and didn't speak for a moment. Finally, she said, "You think Travis and I should date for the same reason you think you and Daniel should date. Right? Just because of some silly plans we made when we were little?"

"They're not silly plans!" I couldn't believe Lacey could have forgotten. "You guys are *perfect* for each other! You've been best friends forever and you know everything about each other!"

"Doesn't mean we should be a couple."

I tried to calm myself down. Maybe Lacey didn't mean that they wouldn't *ever* be a couple. Maybe she just wasn't ready quite yet. "You guys are going to be a couple at *some* point, though, right? Maybe next year?" I said hopefully.

"Honestly, I don't even want a boyfriend until I'm out of high school. Probably even out of college. Having a boyfriend is nothing but a distraction, and I want to focus on my studies. I need to get into Stanford or Harvard."

"But *Travis* wouldn't be a distraction. You hang out with him anyway. Well, you used to."

"I don't like him that way. I like him as a friend, almost a brother. And he likes someone else."

"*What?*" Somehow the news that Travis liked somebody else hit me just as hard as finding out that Daniel liked Madalaine. Maybe even harder, because with Daniel I'd been suspecting it for a while, even though I hadn't wanted to admit it. "Who? Who does he like? What is up with these Malone boys liking girls other than us? Is there something *wrong* with us or something?"

Lacey started laughing. She started laughing so hard she couldn't stop. She almost fell out of her chair, she was laughing so hard.

"What's *wrong* with you?" I demanded.

"N-nothing," Lacey wiped tears of laughter from her eyes. "I just—you're so melodramatic. Just because someone doesn't like you that way doesn't mean something's *wrong* with you."

"Well, seriously. Daniel is supposed to like me, but he likes someone else. Travis is supposed to like you, but he likes someone else. You don't like anyone else and I don't like anyone else, but both of those boys are just… just messing everything up from the way it's supposed to be!"

Lacey calmed down and finally stopped laughing. "Alanna. There is no 'supposed to be'. Life is life. Things change, people change, the things people want change. Everything changes and that's just how it is. Do you know how many kids say they want to marry their parents when they grow up?"

"Ew. Marry their *parents*?"

"Yeah. Lots of little kids—three, four, five years old—say that they want to marry their parents, because they love their parents, and they know that marriage has something to do with love, etcetera etcetera. But obviously, when they get older, they realize, 'ew, that's gross, I don't want to marry my parents, and I couldn't anyway even if I wanted to.'"

"That's different."

Lacey shrugged. "Not really. And do you know how

many kids want to be firefighters and police officers and veterinarians when they're little?"

I knew where she was going with this. "Yeah, I know. A whole bunch, and then most of them end up becoming something else."

"Exactly. Because they change, and they realize that what they used to want isn't what they want anymore. Sooner or later, we all have to grow up, Alanna."

I knew that. I knew I would have to grow up. That's why I was so worried.

Because when I grew up, would anything be the same as it was when I was little? Would Lacey and I still be friends with Travis and Daniel? Would the four of us ever even get to see each other?

Chapter 19

More Basketball

I decided to give Madalaine the benefit of the doubt. It was unlikely, but *maybe* she hadn't known that Daniel and I were supposed to be together. So I decided to be polite to her and not intentionally ignore her like I'd been trying to do for the last couple days. I even started sitting next to her on the bus again, and Daniel went back to sitting with his other friends.

I was glad about that. Daniel was still on my bad list. Daniel had known we were supposed to be together.

Thursday was the day the basketball results were posted. They were posted on a list outside the gym. I went down right before lunch to take a peek. I located my name and my heart did a little flip-flop.

Alanna Fenn..........Level 2 Team (second string)

I'd made it! I'd made it onto the Level 2 team! I was on second string, which meant I wouldn't be one of the starting players. But at least I'd made it onto the real team!

I searched up and down the list, looking for Amanda's name. It was difficult, because I didn't remember her last name until I saw it just a few names above mine:

Amanda Durand…...Level 2 Team (second string)

I cheered. Right there in the hallway area outside the gym, I let out a "Whooo!" and pumped my fist in the air. Then I ran to the lunchroom and found Amanda. "Amanda! We're both on the team!"

"I know!" Amanda grinned and held up her hand for a high-five. "I can't wait till our first practice."

"When's our first practice?"

"Next Monday. It said so on the bottom of the sheet. Our team meets Mondays, Wednesdays, and Fridays, and the Level 1 team meets on Tuesdays and Thursdays."

Mondays, Wednesdays, and Fridays. The days Daniel didn't have programming club. I wasn't sure exactly when student council met—the schedule didn't seem very consistent—but now it didn't matter. I wouldn't have *any* time during the week to spend with Daniel.

Did I care? I wasn't sure.

I couldn't wait to share the good news with Travis after school. When I got home, I put my stuff down in the living room and called to the house at large, "I'm going next door!"

I heard Mom respond, "Okay!" and I left.

It was weird, I reflected as I walked over, that I didn't really have to wonder whether Lacey would already be there. I was pretty sure I knew where she would be. She would be up in her room, or maybe at the kitchen table, working on homework. Not hanging out with the boy who was supposed to be her boyfriend.

I went up to the Malones' door and tried to open it. It didn't budge. I rolled my eyes impatiently and rang the bell, glaring at the door handle. For twelve years of my life, the Malones' house had been like a second home to Lacey and me, and we'd been able to come and go whenever we wanted. Now, this new locked door thing was making the house of my best friends feel like a house belonging to strangers.

I heard footsteps and then Travis answered the door. He looked surprised to see me. "Oh, hey Alanna. Um, Dan's not here right now…"

"I'm not here to see Dan*iel*," I told him, intentionally stressing the last syllable of Daniel's name. How could even Travis be calling him Dan now? "I know he's not here. I'm here to see you."

"Oh," Travis looked even more surprised. "Oh. Okay. Well… you want to come in?"

I looked at him suspiciously, wondering why he was suddenly acting so weird. "Sure," I said cautiously, stepping into the house.

We walked into the kitchen together and Travis asked me, "Do you want, like, an ice water or something? Or we have milk…"

What was I, formal company? "I don't want anything to drink. I wanted to tell you my good news."

"Oh. What's that?" Now Travis seemed more like regular Travis. I was glad.

I smiled. "I made it on the basketball team! The good one! The Level 2 team, not the Level 1 team. I made it on the team!"

"Wow!" Travis held up both of his hands to high-five me and I slapped them hard. "That's awesome! I knew you'd make it. Remember? Remember how I'm the one who said you should try out?"

"Of course. You get all the credit," I teased.

"You're awesome," said Travis.

I grinned at him, then asked, "Do you wanna go out and play basketball right now? In your driveway?"

"Yeah, let's go! You can show me your Level 2 team skills!"

We went out into the garage and Travis got a basketball. Then we headed out to the driveway. "I challenge you to a one-on-one," I said.

"You're on."

Travis threw the ball up in the middle of the driveway and I jumped for it, but he was taller so he tapped it away from me. And then the game was on.

Travis dribbled the ball up the driveway and took a shot at the edge of the grass—about where the foul line would be, if we had one. He missed, so I ran up and caught the rebound. I dribbled back to the grass line—rule was, you had to take it back before you took a shot—and was about to turn around, but Travis took possession of the ball and brought it over near the mailbox. He took another shot, but missed once again and I took the rebound. I brought the ball to the foul line, shot, and scored.

"Seriously," Travis remarked. "Your aim is dead on. You're gonna be the star player on your team."

"I doubt it," I said as I passed the ball in to him. "I'm sure there are girls who've been playing for years and years and years and are way better than me. I'm only on second string."

"Yeah, but after a few games, if you play really well, you'll get moved up to first."

I shrugged. "Maybe."

Travis shot and scored. He passed the ball in to me, and we got back to focusing on the game. We decided it would be a whoever-gets-to-ten-points-first-wins game, and it got pretty intense toward the end. Finally, I pulled off a win.

"Nice job," said Travis, giving me a fist bump. "Hey, so when's your first game? With your team, I mean."

"I have no idea." I flopped on the grass. "*Now* I'm ready for that ice water!"

"Let's go in and get some," said Travis, starting to walk toward the house. He turned around, his face flushed from playing, and made a weird face. "Ice water,

I mean."

I laughed because sometimes Travis said the most obvious things.

We went into the house and filled up glasses of ice water. We drank greedily and filled up our glasses again. Then Travis said, "Let me know when you find out about your first game, okay? I wanna go to it. I wanna see you play."

"Okay." I remembered that Travis had played basketball for his school the year before. "Are you still playing basketball this year? Are you on your school team?"

"Tryouts are next Monday. We'll see. I want to be on it."

"You'll make it," I said, giving him the kind of encouragement he had given me. "I know you will. You're good."

"Thanks, Alanna," said Travis, smiling. "I hope you're right."

We finished our ice waters and sat there in the kitchen for a little bit. Then I asked Travis if he wanted to go out and play again. "After all," I said, grinning teasingly, "What's better practice than playing with the best?"

"I'll show you who's *the best*," said Travis. "Let's go!"

And as we played our second game out in the Malones' driveway, it occurred to me how very glad I was that my basketball practices didn't take place on Tuesdays and Thursdays. Because even though I had to give up hanging out with Daniel, I didn't have to give up playing basketball with Travis.

Chapter 20
Like Old Times, But Not Really

Friday was the first day since Daniel and Madalaine had become a couple that Daniel actually rode home on the bus, rather than staying after school for activities. When we got off at the bus stop together, we both just kind of stood there awkwardly, not sure what to do. A couple weeks ago, I would've just asked Daniel which house we were going to. But now, I wasn't even sure if we were going to the same house.

"So," said Daniel. "Uh, are you going home?"

I shrugged.

"We could hang out a little if you want."

It was beautiful to hear those words. And yet, it wasn't. Because I could tell he was only saying that to be nice to me, not because he really wanted to hang out with me. Wasn't he? He seemed almost apologetic. Like, *I know you really want to hang out with me, so I guess I'll be a good boy and take some time out of my busy schedule to hang out with you for a little bit. Then I'll go back to my life, and you'll go back to yours.*

I shrugged. "Whatever you want to do."

Daniel looked surprised. He probably expected me to be all "Daniel, Daniel, Daniel!" like I was at the beginning of the year. He probably expected me to jump with joy at the idea of finally hanging out with him. But this past week had changed that. His new relationship with Madalaine had changed that. I was done being Daniel's shadow.

"Okay, well… do your rollerblades still fit you? We could rollerblade, like we did last year."

There had been a period of time the year before, back in sixth grade, when Daniel and I had rollerbladed everywhere. We'd gotten the rollerblades for Christmas of fifth grade, but hadn't really used them until sixth grade started. And the first couple months of sixth grade, that was what we'd done every single day after school until it got dark.

When we'd first started on the rollerblades, we'd both been awful. We'd had to hold on to each other to stay up, and sometimes that wouldn't work out and one of us would end up pulling the other down. But eventually we'd gotten the hang of it. And then we got really good on them. We'd roll all around the neighborhood. Sometimes Travis and Lacey would join us on their rollerblades (which they'd also gotten for Christmas), and other times it would just be the two of us. Just me and Daniel.

And now Daniel was offering that again. "Okay," I said. Maybe rollerblading with Daniel again would fix everything. Maybe it would make everything the way it was last year. Maybe, rollerblading with me around the neighborhood just the way we used to, Daniel would remember how good things were back then. And he'd decide to break up with Madalaine and start going out with me. Or at least break up with Madalaine and start spending more *time* with me, and know that *eventually* he'd be going out with me.

We walked home, and each went to our separate

houses to get our rollerblades. "Hi Mom," I said as I walked past her on my way to the living room closet.

"Hi Alanna. How was school today?"

"Fine. I'm going out to rollerblade with Daniel."

"Oh, good! You guys finally have some time to spend together?"

I nodded.

"That's great, I'm glad it's working out. Have fun!"

I gave Mom a hug and headed out the door with my rollerblades. I wasn't sure about how well things were *working out*, what with the whole Madalaine thing and our busy, conflicting schedules, but at least Daniel and I had this time together.

Daniel was sitting on the curb putting his roller-blades on by the time I walked out my front door. I went up and met him. We laced our blades in silence. Then we both stood up, on our own, without any support from each other. Last year, we'd always needed to hold on to each other whenever we stood up from sitting on the ground. This year, we were independent.

"Around the block?" I suggested.

Daniel nodded. We took off.

Our block was fairly flat—a few small hills here and there, but nothing major or dangerous. The next street over had a fairly steep hill, which we'd rollerbladed down a few times last year (and which had given me a scraped elbow and Daniel a skinned knee). But for right now, we were satisfied with just staying on the mostly flat part.

It felt different, rollerblading with Daniel now after all this time. The weirdest thing was that we had nothing to talk about. I thought back to the days I'd spent hanging out with Travis. Travis and I had had a *ton* to talk about. Mostly basketball stuff, but also he had asked me about my classes, and I'd asked him about his high school classes, and he'd told me about what the high school was like and everything. The only moments of silence we'd had were when we were concentrating really hard on playing our game.

But with Daniel, as we skated along, I suddenly couldn't think of anything to say. I didn't want to talk about school or Daniel's friends or Madalaine. Those topics would probably just make Daniel wish he was with them rather than with me. But then what *could* we talk about?

"I made the basketball team," I said, as we rounded the first corner.

"Yeah, I know."

"My first practice is on Monday. Same as Travis's tryouts for his basketball team."

Daniel gave me a weird look. "How do you know when Travis's tryouts are?"

"'Cause he told me. Yesterday when you weren't here. I was playing basketball with him in your driveway."

"Oh." Daniel paused. "Was Lacey there too?"

Was Daniel jealous? Was he finally realizing that he might be missing out on something by getting so involved in school?

I considered telling Daniel that yes, Lacey had been there, and all three of us had had a fantabulous time doing all sorts of fun things together without Daniel. But that wasn't the truth. "No," I said. "She was doing homework."

"Oh." Daniel looked a little relieved, and that made me happy. So he *did* miss us, a little bit. He *would* have been jealous if all three of us had been hanging out without him.

We skated in silence for a little while longer. We reached the end of our block, where we had the option to go back to our houses, take the same loop again, or continue on to the street with the big hill.

"Which way do you want to go?" I asked Daniel.

He shrugged. "Let's just go around the loop again. I'm out of practice. I feel like I'd fall if I went down that hill."

So we took the same loop again, and then a third time, and even though we weren't really talking much, it was kind of like old times. Just me and Daniel, roller-blading together.

Until we got home from our third loop, and I asked Daniel if we were going around again. "Well…" he said, "I was kind of planning on going in now. Just… you know. I'm getting tired, and I promised Tyler I'd check Instagram for a picture he said he was gonna post."

I remembered that these weren't the old times and that nothing was the same now. "*Tyler?* I thought you didn't even like him."

Daniel shrugged. "He can be kind of a jerk sometimes, but he's still part of the group. He took a picture of Maddie and me in science today and I wanna see how it came out."

I nodded, trying to hide my disappointment. "Okay," I said. "Well, it's a free country. You can do what you want."

Daniel gave me a look that implied that he thought

I was being unreasonable. "Hey, come on. We just had a nice time rollerblading together. And you even said, back at the bus stop, that you didn't care whether I went home or hung out with you. I just hung out with you, now I'm going to go check Instagram. Okay?"

I mentally cursed myself for ruining a perfectly nice afternoon with Daniel. Of course Daniel didn't *have* to be out here rollerblading with me. He could have gone home and checked his Instagram from the start. I shouldn't be making such a big deal about Daniel having other friends.

"Sorry," I told him, and I honestly meant it. "Of course it's okay. I didn't mean to be such a jerk about it. It's just—of all people, *Tyler?*"

"Once you get to know him he's not too bad."

"If you say so."

"You should start eating lunch with us again. Then you'll get to know everyone better, and they'll get to know you, and yeah. It'll be better that way."

Daniel started heading over to his house, and for the first time since he'd said he was going home, I smiled. Because Daniel had actually asked me to start eating lunch with him and his friends again, which meant that things couldn't be as bad as they had seemed.

172

Chapter 21

The Weekend

Saturday afternoon found me changing out my summer clothes for winter clothes. I'd wanted to go over to the Malones' house—preferably with Lacey—and see if Travis and Daniel could do something with us. But Mom and Dad had insisted that since we were really starting to get into fall, it was going to start getting colder, so we needed to switch warm clothes into our drawers and closets and cooler clothes into bags to put in the hall closet until spring.

Dad was letting me use his iPad for music as I worked, so I was blaring Taylor Swift songs from You-Tube. Actually, I was blaring *a* Taylor Swift song from

YouTube. "You Belong With Me" over and over again. I liked the song because I could relate to it. Taylor was singing about how her best friend should be dating her, but he's actually dating some other girl. Exactly like me and Daniel and Madalaine. Of course, Madalaine was nothing like the girl in the music video, but it was still a similar story.

I sang along as I placed a pile of T-shirts in a bag for the hall closet: "If you could see that I'm the one who understands you..."

But how well *did* I understand Daniel? It was true that I *used* to know everything about him. But now...what did Daniel do in his spare time, when he wasn't with me? He hung out with Madalaine and Hunter and Max and I guess Tyler, but what did he actually *do* with them? Did they ever rollerblade together, in someone else's neighborhood? Did they ever play Wii together? Did any of them have a tree fort like Daniel and I did? Did they ever spend time together doing pretty much nothing, just enjoying being together?

And did Daniel still like me (as a friend), or had he only hung out with me on Friday to be nice?

These were the kinds of things I was thinking about as I cleaned out my drawers. I had just taken a sweater out of a hall-closet bag when I heard the door-bell ring.

I jumped up. My confused feelings about Daniel didn't change the excitement I felt at the possibility that he might be the one at the door. It was unlikely, I knew. But there was still a chance…

I started running downstairs just as Dad was opening the door. "Hi Travis," Dad said. "You here for Lacey?"

"Uh, no," said Travis, looking down and to the side. "Um… is Alanna here?"

"She is, but—"

"I'm here," I jumped down the last few steps and landed next to Dad. "Hi Travis!"

Dad looked at me. "Are you done switching out your clothes?"

"Almost." I was about halfway through and my room was a mess. But halfway was better than nothing. I was closer to being done than I'd been when I first started.

"Well, if you're in the middle of doing something, I don't want to interrupt that," Travis said quickly.

"No, I can finish later." Why was Travis here looking for *me*? Dad had specifically asked if Travis wanted

175

to see Lacey, and Travis had said no. He was here to see me. I smiled up at Dad in what I hoped was a charming, innocent manner. "Right, Dad?"

Dad gave me a look. "If you really will finish later."

"I will. I promise I will."

"Okay then." Dad went back toward the kitchen, and Travis and I were left facing each other in the doorway.

"Um," said Travis, looking down at his feet and sort of half-laughing. "I mean, if you have something else to do, I don't want to take you away from that. I was just wondering if… maybe you'd like to come out and help me practice for tryouts? Just, you know, shoot around a little, maybe do a little scrimmage or something? If you want." He looked up and met my eyes, but his expression still looked weird. Uncertain.

He was acting like he thought I was going to say no. He was acting like inviting me outside to play basketball was a really difficult thing to do, like I was going to slam the door in his face or something. Why?

"All I was doing was switching out my summer clothes and winter clothes. Bo-ring! I'd definitely rather play basketball with you. Let's go." I hopped down onto the front step and shut the door behind me.

The basketball was already sitting out on Travis's driveway, so we ran over and he picked it up and passed it to me. I started dribbling it, then took a shot, which missed. Travis took the rebound and made the basket.

"See, just me being here is making you a better player," I teased. "I don't even have to do anything!"

"Oh yeah?" Travis passed the ball to me. "Maybe I should practice with you all the time, then."

"You should." I took a shot and it went in.

"So what were some of the drills you did in your tryouts?" Travis asked me.

"Girls' tryouts at the junior high?" I gave him a look, implying that his boys' tryouts at the high school were probably going to be very different. "We did some layups, foul shots, dribbling, passing, and guarding. A little bit of everything. Why?"

"Just trying to get an idea."

"Weren't you on the basketball team when you were in junior high?"

"Yeah, but tryouts were back in *seventh grade*. That was two years ago."

It suddenly struck me as weird that Travis was two years older than me, and he and I were getting along better than Daniel and I were. It was too bad, I reflect-

to the net, sinking the basket flawlessly.

"Enough with layups," I said. "Let's do a passing drill now."

"Okay, boss."

We had just gotten into the passing drill when the front door opened and Daniel came out. I hadn't even known he was home. To be honest, I hadn't thought about him at all since Travis had come over.

"Hi Daniel," I said. "Wanna join us?"

"No, that's okay." Daniel stood watching us. "Just coming out to see what you guys were doing."

"I'm helping Travis get ready for tryouts," I said.

"Mm." Daniel nodded. He stayed out for a couple more minutes and then went back in.

I felt a little bad. Had he wanted to do something with me? Or with both of us? We could have stopped our practicing and done something that would interest him.

"All right, now it's crazy shot time," Travis said, widening his eyes and stretching his grin to make his whole face look crazy. "Here I go!" He stood at the grass line and took a shot—backward. The ball bounced off the rim and right to me.

"All right! Score! I meant to do it like that," he

joked.

I smiled. "Okay. My turn." I went out to the street and did an underhand "bowling" shot. The ball didn't make it anywhere near the net. We both cracked up.

And as Travis went to grab the ball and take his next crazy shot, I realized that I didn't care that Daniel hadn't joined us, or that we hadn't invited him to do anything else with us. I didn't even care, at the moment, that I might not get to hang out with Daniel at all this weekend.

I was having more fun with Travis anyway.

Chapter 22

The First Practice

"Ready for our first practice?" Amanda asked me in FCS class on Monday as we gathered the ingredients for French toast. We'd finished the sewing projects on Friday, and it was finally time to start cooking stuff.

"Yep!" I didn't tell her that it technically wasn't my *first* practice, because of practicing with Travis. I'd spent practically all day Saturday, and a decent amount of Sunday, playing basketball with him. I didn't know what Daniel was doing all that time. And I didn't really think about it much.

"Hey, Alanna, you have basketball practice and Dan and I have student council," said Madalaine. "Maybe we'll all ride home together on the late bus!"

"You guys are lucky," commented Shelly. "You all get to do something fun after school today. I have to go to my little cousins' house. They're two and four, and they're super whiny."

"Well, I have something to cheer you up," said Amanda. "All three of you. My parents said I could have a sleepover next Friday. You guys are all invited."

A sleepover? It would be my very first sleepover with anyone other than Lacey and the Malones. Daniel had already had his. Now I'd be catching up.

"What time do you want us to come?" I asked.

"I'm thinking around six or seven. We're going to order pizza for dinner and then stay up as late as we want."

Amanda, Shelly, and Madalaine kept talking about the sleepover as we made our French toast, and I just listened and tried to gather information. I didn't know what girls did at junior high school sleepovers, and I didn't want to ask because they'd all think I was stupid for not knowing. At the sleepovers Lacey and I had had with Daniel and Travis, we'd done kind of what we regularly did—invented imaginary worlds, played Wii, played hide-and-seek, listened to music, watched movies, ate snacks—and then had the occasional pillow fight or, when we were younger, tackle game. But somehow I didn't think those were the kinds of things we'd be doing at Amanda's sleepover.

The bell rang for the end of school, and Amanda and I left class together and headed toward the gym. "I wonder what practice will be like," she commented.

I shrugged. "I guess we'll find out." I wondered what Travis's tryouts would be like. I crossed my fingers and prayed that he would do well.

Coach Davison—the same one who'd run the tryouts—blew his whistle to start practice. He lined us all up on the bleachers and told us what we were going to do—a bunch of drills (basically the same ones I'd done with Travis), and then a scrimmage. He split us up into two groups to do the drills, one on each side of the gym. I wasn't in Amanda's group.

The first drill was layups. I lined up with a bunch of girls I didn't know. Well, technically I *knew* a couple of them. There was one girl I'd known from elementary school, named Samantha. There were a few girls from my classes, but I didn't really remember their names.

As the first few girls took their layups, I started feeling kind of self-conscious. I was really bad at layups.

What if I was the first one to miss? Or what if I missed all the shots I took?

I thought back to when I'd been practicing with Travis, and exactly how he'd positioned my hands on the ball before I'd taken my shot. If I could just do it that same way, then maybe…

"Hey, what are you grinning about?" a girl asked me. "You just missed the pass."

A couple girls laughed. I realized that I had, in fact, missed the ball that had just been passed to me. It was rolling across the floor. *Well, it must not have been a very good pass*, I thought, annoyed.

I went and got the ball. I could feel everyone's eyes watching me. I started dribbling it, pretending nothing had happened. I dribbled it up to the net and took the shot exactly the way Travis had taught me.

It went in!

I passed the ball to the next girl and went to the back of the line. It would be fine now, if I missed a couple other layups. At least I'd made my first one.

We finished the layup drill, and then did passing, dribbling with obstacles, and various shooting drills. Then we did the scrimmage, with our teams being the same groups we'd been in for the drills. I wasn't starting, but that was good because I could watch my team-mates. I analyzed the way they played, watching who was best at handling the ball, who was best at passing, who was best at shooting, etcetera etcetera etcetera.

When it was my turn to go in, I played my hardest. The competition was tough—some of the girls were a lot better than me. But I was at least able to make a couple baskets.

By the time practice was over, I was exhausted. But I dragged my body into the locker room with all the other girls, and then outside to get on the late bus. A bunch of other kids were also waiting for the late bus—kids from other activities that had gotten out earlier than our practice. "When does the late bus even come?" I asked Amanda.

She shrugged. "I have no idea. My dad always picks me up. Actually, I see him right now. Bye!" She started jogging over to a silver minivan, leaving me alone with all these girls I didn't know. Some of whom weren't very nice.

Man, I could really use a cell phone right now! I thought. If I had a cell phone, I could just call Mom or Dad and ask them to pick me up.

Just as I was thinking this, and feeling sorry for

myself, I heard, "Alanna!"

I turned around to see both Daniel and Madalaine walking out of the building, waving at me. I felt relief crash over me. I wouldn't have to go home on the late bus alone!

I started walking toward them and met them halfway. "How was practice?" Madalaine asked me.

"Good," I said. "I made some shots."

"Awesome! Student council was good too. We started planning a school dance."

"A school dance?"

"Yeah. End of October. It'll sort of be a Halloween dance, except it won't be on Halloween because we don't want it to interfere with trick-or-treating, and we were kind of having an argument about whether people should come in costume or not. I thought yes, but some other people were saying no, and we didn't really come to a definite decision."

I scrunched up my nose and made myself ask the question. "Are you two going to the dance together?"

"Um, the teachers were saying it shouldn't really be a partner dance," said Madalaine. "So no kids would feel left out for not having a partner. But a lot of kids are going with partners anyway."

"So…" said Daniel. "Madalaine, do you want to go with me? As my partner?"

Madalaine giggled and grabbed Daniel's arm with both of her hands. "Yes," she said, looking in his eyes, and once again it was like I wasn't there.

It still hurt, seeing them together like that. Knowing Daniel was supposed to be mine. But I forced myself to remember that Madalaine probably didn't know that. After all, I'd said "no" when she'd asked if I was upset about her and Daniel dating. And Daniel probably thought along the same lines as Lacey—that just because we'd planned our marriage in kindergarten, that didn't mean it was actually going to happen.

"So…what else did you do in student council?" I asked, just to get their focus on something other than each other.

"Not much," said Madalaine, shrugging. "Just pretty much planned the dance. Hey, we should all go to the dance together. Me and Daniel and you and your partner."

"Me and *my partner*?" Somehow it made me happy that Madalaine thought I would have a partner. It also kind of made me laugh. Where would I find a partner for this dance, if I couldn't go with Daniel? I didn't have any other boy friends at school. "Who am I supposed to go with?"

"I don't know. Who do you like?"

Daniel, I wanted to say. But what would happen if I said that? Daniel would probably get mad at me. And Madalaine would probably be confused, or sad, or upset or something. And maybe they would break up, which would be good, except... it wouldn't. Because if they broke up because of me, they'd be sad and maybe mad at me and I'd feel bad for causing their sadness. And, I hated to admit it, but them breaking up wouldn't automatically mean Daniel and me being together.

So I just shrugged and said, "No one."

"Well, you could go with one of our friends," said Daniel. "Maybe Hunter? Max? I know you don't like Tyler."

I didn't really like Max or Hunter either. They treated me like an outsider. But it was nice that Madalaine and Daniel were at least trying to get me to join them at the dance.

"Maybe," I finally said. "I'll decide later."

"Well, even if you don't have a partner, you should definitely come," said Madalaine. "It would be so much more fun with you there."

189

"Yeah," agreed Daniel. "You should come either way."

The bus pulled up, and we boarded: Madalaine and me together in our normal seats, and Daniel right in front of us. Daniel and Madalaine mainly talked about stuff that had happened in their student council meeting, so I didn't get to contribute much to the conversation, but for some reason, this time I didn't really mind.

It was enough that I was with my friends.

Chapter 23

Almost Ruined

When we got off at the bus stop, I followed Daniel to his house instead of going to mine. "Oh..." he said when he realized I was following him. "Um, I was kinda gonna do some stuff for student council? Like, it's sort of like homework, and I feel like if I wait I'm gonna forget about it, so..."

I realized what he was implying. He thought I was following him because I wanted to hang out with him. Funny how that thought hadn't even crossed my mind.

"That's fine," I said quickly. "I'm just following you because I want to talk to Travis."

"Oh," Daniel looked surprised. "O-Okay."

We found Travis in the living room, watching TV. I told him about my practice, and asked him about his tryouts. "I'm pretty sure I made the team," he said. "I wasn't doing so hot at first, but then I started pretending I was out in the driveway with you, just being crazy and throwing stuff around, and I started doing better."

"Hey! That's what I did too! Well, kind of. We'd better practice a lot tomorrow, to keep our skills sharp."

Travis gave me a thumbs-up. "You got it."

I wanted to go right over to the Malones' after school the next day, but I needed to drop my stuff off at home first. I opened the front door, intending just to stick my backpack inside and call out that I was home, but I stopped when I heard voices coming from the kitchen.

I went inside to see what was up. To my surprise, Lacey was sitting at the kitchen table, *not* on her laptop or surrounded by a pile of books. Instead, she was surrounded by people. Two boys and a girl, all sitting around eating popcorn and apple slices.

"Whoa… what's going on here?" I asked.

"Oh, hi Alanna," said Lacey, looking up and waving. "These are some of my friends. Hannah, Jason, and Keyan."

Hannah smiled at me. Jason nodded. Keyan waved.

"What are you guys doing?" I asked.

"Just hanging out," said Lacey. "We're all so busy with homework, and after-school activities are starting up, so we figured we'd take a little time just to hang out together today."

There was something wrong with this. Lacey never had time to just "hang out" with me and Travis and Daniel anymore—or at least with me and Travis, since Daniel was always busy too. But she had time to hang out with these friends?

"Where's Travis?" I asked. "Why isn't he with you guys?"

"He's at his house, waiting for you. I thought you guys were going to play basketball."

It made me happy that Travis remembered, and that he really did want to play basketball with me. But there was still something wrong with the fact that he wasn't with Lacey. And I didn't really like the way Keyan was looking at Lacey. It reminded me of the way Daniel looked at Madalaine.

"Maybe you could come over too?" I suggested. "All of you? We could do teams."

"We're going to stay here for now," said Lacey.

"You go have fun with Travis."

I sighed. "*Fine.*"

I turned around and went back out the door. It didn't take a genius to see what was happening. Lacey and Travis were drifting apart, just like Daniel and me. I couldn't let that happen. As long as Lacey and Travis got together, I could keep the hope that someday Daniel and I would still get together, and everything would be like we'd always planned.

Even if I didn't fully believe it.

I trudged through the grass over to the Malones' house. I didn't even try the door this time. I knew it would be locked. Instead, I rang the bell. A few seconds later, Travis opened the door.

"Hey. Ready for some basketball?"

"Yeah."

"I'll go get the ball." Travis disappeared into the house and returned a few moments later with his basketball. We headed out to the driveway and started shooting hoops.

After a couple minutes, I got up the courage to start the conversation I should have started weeks ago. "I need to talk to you about something important."

"Oh yeah?" said Travis, getting ready to aim for a

three-pointer. "What's that?"

"Lacey," I said forcefully.

Travis looked surprised. Evidently, this was not what he'd been expecting. "What about her?" he asked, bringing his arms down and holding the ball.

"More specifically, *you* and Lacey," I said.

"What's going on with me and Lacey?" Travis looked befuddled.

"Nothing!" I exploded. "*Nothing's* going on with you and Lacey! That's the problem! That's why I need to talk to you about her! She's all like, 'I'm trying to focus only on my studies, I don't need a boyfriend', but I'm sure she'd feel differently if *you* were her boyfriend..." I looked at him pleadingly.

Travis was looking at me with an odd expression on his face. Then, he abruptly turned away and started bouncing the basketball, walking away from me. "Lacey and I don't like each other that way," he said. "Neither of us do. Lacey knows who I like, and she's okay with it."

My heart sank, because Travis had just confirmed what Lacey had told me the week before. That the reason he didn't want to go out with Lacey was because he liked someone else.

"Maybe she isn't really okay with it," I said, just because I wanted him to re-think things a little. "Maybe she was just saying that because she didn't want to hurt your feelings. I bet if you actually start dating the girl you like, Lacey'll be really mad. Just like I was at Daniel." Travis was still dribbling away from me. I was getting impatient. "Will you just shoot the ball already?"

Travis took a shot and missed. I ran up for the rebound and grabbed it, surprised that I hadn't had to fight Travis for it. I looked over and he was still standing by the house, though now he was facing me.

"Well, lucky for you, I probably won't ever get to find out how Lacey would feel if I started dating the girl I like," he said irritably. "Because it's never in a million years going to happen! *She's* the one who'd be mad if I told her I liked her."

"Don't tell her, then."

"I won't." Travis was practically glaring at me. Suddenly I wished I'd never brought the subject up. What was he getting so mad at *me* for? Just because I'd said that Lacey might actually like him?

I tossed the ball and sank a basket. Travis didn't cheer. He didn't say anything.

"Are you mad at me?" I finally asked.

"No." His answer was short and aimed at the

ground. "I just… life gets frustrating, Alanna. How you feel about Daniel, how you can't be his girlfriend because you know he likes someone else? I'm in the same place." He sighed. "I don't want to talk about it."

I didn't want to talk about it either. "Maybe we could just play basketball?" I suggested.

Travis gave me a pained smile. "Yeah. Let's just play basketball." He walked over and picked up the ball, which had rolled over near the garage. He tossed it to me and I started dribbling.

I took a shot, and this time Travis came over and we both tried to get the rebound. He nabbed it, and then I chased him down the driveway as he took it back. And things were back to normal.

But I knew, even as I walked home an hour later, that I wasn't going to try bringing up those subjects again—anything about Lacey or how she and Travis should be boyfriend and girlfriend or about the girl Travis liked. That conversation had almost messed up our afternoon together.

And I didn't want to mess up our afternoons together for anything.

Chapter 24

Almost...

The next time I went over to play basketball with Travis, things were all good again. We didn't talk about Lacey. We didn't talk about the girl Travis liked, or about anything relating to boyfriends or girlfriends. We stayed on "safe" topics—basketball, homework, TV shows, funny things we'd heard people say, which popular songs we liked and which ones we found annoying. And every moment we spent together, I could feel myself getting closer and closer to Travis, and farther and farther from Daniel.

Travis was becoming my new best friend.

I didn't get to hang out with anyone over the weekend, because it was Columbus Day weekend and my parents and Lacey and I went to visit my grandparents. But on Tuesday, as soon as school was over, I smiled my way to the bus.

"You're in a really good mood today," Madalaine commented.

"I get to play basketball with Travis when I get home," I told her. "You know, Daniel's brother. He and I play basketball together every day after school, unless one of us has practice." Travis had told me on Friday that he'd made his school team.

"That's cool," said Madalaine. "I guess that helps you keep up your skills even when you don't have actual basketball practice. Plus, it's always fun doing stuff with friends."

"Yeah," I agreed.

"Are you going to Amanda's sleepover on Friday?"

Oh yeah. Amanda's sleepover. Somehow, I kept forgetting to ask Mom and Dad if I could go. "I still have to ask my parents," I confessed. "But I want to." I hesitated. "So... I've never actually been to a sleepover before, other than with Daniel and Travis and Lacey. What... what exactly do people *do* at, you know, regular sleepovers?"

Madalaine shrugged. "Every one is different, I guess. The ones I've been to, we usually stay up really late and tell stories and share secrets and eat a lot of junk food. We might watch a movie or play a game. I guess it really depends on what we *want* to do."

"Okay," I felt slightly better knowing a little bit about what we might do. It didn't sound too different from the sleepovers I'd had with Daniel and Travis and Lacey. "I'll try to remember to ask my parents tonight. I'm sure they'll say yes."

Madalaine and I talked all the way home, and then we got to my bus stop. "See you tomorrow!" I called to Madalaine.

"Have fun playing basketball with Travis!" she called back to me.

I was still smiling as I walked up my driveway. I could already see Travis in his yard, but he wasn't dribbling the basketball. It looked like he was raking leaves. I dropped my stuff off at home and then ran over to meet him. "Hey."

"Hi." He made an apologetic face. "Sorry, I can't play basketball just yet. My parents said they wanted me to get all these leaves raked before they get home."

I shrugged. "No problem. Can I help?"

"Sure, if you want to. We have another rake in the garage."

I ran to Travis's garage and found the rake. I came back over and joined him in raking the leaves into a big pile toward the back of the yard.

"You know what we're going to have to do when we're done raking," I said after a couple minutes.

"What's that?"

I grinned. "Jump in the leaf pile, obviously! At least once or twice."

Travis grinned too. "Yeah! Just like we used to when we were little." He headed over near the oak tree at the edge of the yard, still raking. "You know, that's one of the things that I find so fun about hanging out with you. You still like doing a lot of the things we did when we were little. Lacey and, like, everyone at high school has kind of outgrown that stuff. Or at least they pretend they have."

"Stinks for them," I said as I added to the pile. "Just 'cause we did it when we were little doesn't mean we can't do it now that we're older."

"Yeah," agreed Travis. "It's still fun."

We kept raking all the leaves in the yard until we had a massive pile out back. It was nearly as tall as I was. "Okay," I said. "Ready? On the count of three. One... two... *three!*"

Travis and I both ran as fast as we could and flung ourselves into the leaf pile. I went at least a couple feet under, with leaves crashing down on top of me. I popped up, laughing. "That was awesome!"

"Let's do it again," said Travis.

We raked up the pile again and went back to our starting place. Again, we ran at the pile, then jumped and soared what felt like a couple feet before falling into the spongy bed of leaves. "Again!" I exclaimed.

We did that over and over, running, jumping, raking, then running and jumping again. We did it until we were lying in the leaf pile, out of breath.

"That was fun," panted Travis.

"Yeah," I agreed. I stared up into the blue sky, partially obscured by the branches of the trees. "It's like the perfect fall day."

"Agreed," said Travis. "And this is the perfect way to spend a perfect fall day."

I smiled. I watched as the wind picked up some leaves and started blowing them around in the sky. "Hey, look! It's raining leaves!" I sat up, tossing a handful of leaves into the air. "It's raining leaves!"

Travis sat up too. "Yeah, nice job getting those leaves in my face, Alanna."

I took one look at him and burst out laughing.

"What? What's so funny?"

"You have leaves sticking up all over your hair! You look like a rooster!"

Travis grinned too. "Well, so do you! We look like King and Queen Leaf." He reached over and started brushing the leaves out of my hair. I couldn't move. I didn't want to move.

Travis brushed a couple more leaves out of my hair and then stopped, his hand at the back of my neck. He looked at me and I looked at him. Then, slowly, he leaned a little closer.

My heart was suddenly pounding like crazy. I leaned closer too.

Travis leaned in closer. And closer. And closer. And—

I jumped up and took off running as fast as I could.

Chapter 25

Thoughts

That wasn't supposed to happen!

The thought pounded at me as I ran blindly home, not watching where I was going, not seeing anything at all except Travis's face growing nearer and nearer, not hearing anything but my still-pounding heart. I flew into my house and up to my room, where I shut and locked the door. Then I crawled under my covers to the very foot of my bed, where I curled into a ball, breathing heavily.

I never wanted to come out.

I did not want to let myself think about what had just almost happened. What just *had* happened. I tried to think of other things instead. Birds. Butterflies. Basket-balls. Musical instruments. But my thoughts kept re-directing and coming around to the undeniable truth.

Travis had tried to kiss me.

And I had almost let him.

The question was *why*? *Why* had Travis tried to kiss me? And even more importantly, why had I almost let him? Travis wasn't Daniel. I wasn't supposed to like him that way. I *didn't* like him that way... right?

Wait. Did this mean that Travis *did* like me that way? Was *I* the girl he'd been talking about, the one who he was so sure didn't like him in the same way, the reason he wasn't interested in Lacey? The one who he thought would be angry if she found out he liked her?

The pieces were slowly forming together in my brain. It all made sense—the reason he'd seemed kind of mad at me the day I'd been bugging him about getting together with Lacey... the reason he'd been practically glaring at me when I told him not to tell the girl he liked that he liked her... the reason he hadn't wanted to discuss that topic with me.

So Travis liked me. *Why*? Why would he like me rather than Lacey?

There was a knock at my door. I jumped. "Alanna?" It was Lacey's voice.

I didn't want to talk to her. I didn't want to talk to anyone. I stayed silent.

"Alanna, are you in there?"

I still didn't answer. Eventually, I heard Lacey's feet walking away, leaving me alone with my thoughts.

Why did Travis like me? What was I supposed to do now?

I stayed under my covers for a long time. I don't know how long it was before there was another knock on the door. I ignored it again.

"Alanna?" It was Lacey again. I heard her rattling the doorknob. "Alanna, you're about to get a text from Travis."

What? I whipped the covers off of me. "I don't have a phone."

"I know. He's sending it to my phone."

Had Travis told Lacey about what had happened? That would be embarrassing. I went over and opened the door.

"Here," said Lacey, handing her phone to me. Her face didn't give away anything.

I looked down at the screen. *Hi Lacey, can you let*

Alanna borrow your phone for a minute? The next text is for her.

As I was reading the text that was already there, another one came in: *Alanna, I'm sorry.*

"What's he sorry for?" Lacey asked, reading over my shoulder. "Did you guys have a fight or something? Is that why you ran home and slammed your door and have been hiding in your room ever since?"

"We didn't have a fight," I mumbled. Somehow, the apology made me feel worse. Was he sorry for trying to kiss me? Was he saying he shouldn't have done it? Was he saying maybe that it had been an accident, maybe that he didn't like me after all?

I handed the phone back to Lacey.

"You can respond," she told me. "You can text him back on my phone. Or call him."

I shook my head.

"Can I at least tell him you read the text?"

I nodded.

"Do you want to talk to me about what happened?"

I shook my head.

"Okay..." Lacey looked like she wanted to help me, but didn't know how. I finally just closed the door and went back to my bed.

A couple minutes later, Lacey spoke through the door. "He says it was all his fault and he should've taken your advice and he hopes you're not mad at him but understands if you are. Alanna, what the heck *happened* today? What did Travis do?"

I didn't answer. I wasn't mad at him. I was just confused.

Did he like me?

What advice had I given him?

Why was he apologizing?

"Okay, I get it. You don't want to talk right now. I'll leave you alone. But can you at least tell me what to tell Travis?"

I kept the covers up over my face. I didn't know what I wanted to tell him. I didn't know how I felt about him, or about what had just happened, or about anything at all.

"Tell him I'm not mad."

Chapter 26

The Sleepover

My routine went back to boring. I didn't want to go to Travis's house after school, because it would be too awkward. What were we supposed to say to each other? What were we supposed to do? Even if we just played basketball, the scene from the day before would keep creeping back into my mind. I'd want to ask him questions. And what if the answers weren't what I wanted to hear?

The next morning I met Daniel at the bus stop. He had his phone out and it looked like he was texting somebody.

"Who're you texting?" I asked, just to make conversation.

"Madalaine," he replied, not looking up.

I nodded. Somehow, this didn't make me jealous at all. Daniel was allowed to have friends other than me. Even a girlfriend. And even if he kissed Madalaine right in front of me, I couldn't get mad. After all, I had almost let Travis kiss me.

That was the part that was hardest to think about. I'd known what was happening. I'd known what he was about to do. I'd even leaned forward for the kiss.

Did that mean I liked Travis?

The bus pulled up and Daniel and I got on. Daniel joined Hunter, and I sat in my usual seat next to Madalaine.

"Look at this," she exclaimed, holding her phone so I could see the screen. "Daniel just sent me this. Were you there when he sent it? Isn't it cute?"

The picture on the screen was of two pandas hugging each other. Underneath the picture, Daniel's text read *Me and you.*

I was aware of how weird it was that I felt nothing as I looked at the text and the picture. No jealousy. No anger. No frustration. "That is cute," I agreed.

The week dragged by. It was only a four-day school

week—well, three, really, after Tuesday—but it felt longer because I had nothing to look forward to after school. Sure, I had a couple basketball practices, but they were only for an hour each. When I got home, I had nothing to do but sit in my room, watching YouTube videos or drawing listlessly or staring at the ceiling. I was so glad when Friday finally came, because on Friday I actually did have something to look forward to.

Amanda's sleepover. I'd asked my parents if I could go, and they'd said yes. So Friday afternoon, after practice, I went into my room not to mope around, but to pack.

I had no idea what to pack.

"Lacey!" Lacey was working on homework in her room and had told everyone not to bother her, but this was an emergency. "Lacey!"

"What?"

"Come into my room!"

A few seconds later, Lacey came into my room, looking irritated. "Why do I have to come into your room?"

"Because I don't know what to pack for my friend's sleepover," I said sheepishly. "Like, should I pack pajamas? My friends told me that people don't really *sleep* much at sleepovers, but should I bring them anyway? And should I bring, I don't know, anything else?"

Lacey's irritated face smoothed out into a look of compassion. "Oh, Alanna... you've been to sleepovers before. The ones we used to have, you and me and Travis and Daniel? Regular sleepovers aren't much different from that."

My heart did a somersault when she said Travis's name. I tried not to let anything show. "Are you sure?" I asked.

"Yes, I'm sure. Bring your pajamas, bring your toothbrush, go look through the pantry and see if you can find any pretzels or chips or candy or anything to bring, and that's it. You don't really need anything else."

By five-thirty, I was in the backseat of the car, and Dad was driving me over to Amanda's house. "My little girl's first sleepover!" he said, grinning at me in the rearview mirror.

"Kind of," I corrected him.

"Well, aside from the ones you guys used to have with Daniel and Travis," he amended.

Once again, I felt something in my chest when he said Travis's name. What was Travis doing right now?

Was he thinking about me? Had he missed me at all this week?

We pulled into Amanda's driveway, and Dad insisted on coming up to the door with me and meeting Amanda's parents. Madalaine and Shelly were both already there, so I went and talked with them and Amanda while the parents chatted. Then Dad gave me a hug and kiss goodbye, and the sleepover actually began.

"So," said Amanda, leading us down the stairs. "We're sleeping in the basement tonight, since it has more room than my bedroom, and so we're farther away from my parents' and brothers' rooms. This way we can be loud and stuff." She showed us the basement, which was big and open and carpeted.

"Um," I said, as I realized something neither Lacey nor I had thought of. "Were we supposed to bring sleeping bags?"

"I have a bunch of sleeping bags," Amanda assured me. "And blankets and pillows. We go camping a lot, so yeah, we're well-stocked." She walked over to a bookshelf in the corner, which was full of all sorts of board games. "You guys wanna play a game before dinner?"

We ended up playing Apples to Apples, and then Scrabble, and then it was time for dinner. We ate pizza with Amanda's parents and two older brothers, then went back down to the basement, where we had a dancing contest (Madalaine won), an arm-wrestling tournament (Amanda won) and a pillow fight (we all got bopped in the head so many times, it was impossible to tell who won!). Around eleven, Amanda's mom came down and told us to tone it down a little because the rest of the family was going to bed.

"Let's set up the sleeping bags and, like, tell secrets or something," said Amanda. So we all took turns in the bathroom putting our pajamas on, and then set up our sleeping bags and blankets and pillows in a circle on the floor, with all of our heads facing inward so we could talk.

"Any secrets?" Shelly asked, looking around at all of us. Nobody answered, and then we all started giggling.

"It's not a secret, but it's something exciting," said Madalaine. "Daniel and I have been together for two and a half weeks now!"

"Awwwww," said Shelly. "You guys are so cute together."

"Yeah, you are," Amanda agreed.

To my surprise, I found myself nodding along with them. Daniel and Madalaine *did* make a good couple.

214

And somehow, it no longer bothered me that they were together.

"Have you guys, like—" Shelly broke off and giggled. Then she leaned closer. "Have you guys, like, you know, kissed yet?"

Madalaine giggled too. "No, but we have held hands. Three times! We haven't really been dating long enough to kiss."

"Yeah, and plus you mainly just see each other at school, and school isn't a great place for kissing," added Amanda.

Madalaine looked around the circle. "Has anyone here ever kissed a boy before?"

My heart started pounding as I pictured what had happened Tuesday afternoon.

"I did, in first grade," said Shelly. "But that doesn't really count."

"I never have," said Amanda.

Everybody looked at me.

"Um," I said, feeling my face start to get hot. "I… almost did. Or, well, a boy almost kissed me. Three days ago."

My friends all squealed and leaned forward. "Ohmygosh, *who*?" asked Amanda.

"No one you guys know," I said quickly. "My… friend. From my neighborhood."

"Wait, so how did he *almost* kiss you?" asked Shelly.

I could feel my face getting even warmer. "Well… he was going to, but I…um, I ran away."

My friends burst into giggles. "I'm so sorry," said Amanda. "It's really not funny. We shouldn't be laughing. Do you like him?"

I thought about all the fun I'd had with Travis, playing basketball in his driveway, jumping in the leaves, taking the bike ride, and all the times before that. Times when we were with Daniel and Lacey, just hanging out and having fun. I remembered how I'd felt when he was standing behind me, helping me do a layup—that kind of nervous/excited feeling, and how I'd smiled whenever I thought back to the memory. I remembered how I'd felt when Lacey told me Travis was interested in someone else—not knowing that "someone else" was me—and how it had hit me even harder than finding out that Daniel liked Madalaine.

Maybe I had always liked Travis, but had never wanted to admit it, because I'd been so stuck on feeling like I *should* like Daniel.

Slowly, I nodded. It was weird admitting it. But it

was the truth.

"So what are you going to do?" asked Shelly.

Good question. "I haven't figured that part out yet," I told her.

"Why'd you run away?" asked Amanda.

That was another good question. I thought about it before answering. "I guess I was scared," I finally said. "And… confused, because I'd always thought I liked someone else… but I really do like him."

"Then you should kiss him," said Shelly, grinning. "Just a suggestion."

"Or at least talk to him about it," said Amanda.

I shrugged. "I'll let you know if I do."

The conversation trailed off, and then we started talking about Shelly's nail polish. We ended up painting all of our nails, then watching a movie, then playing Telephone, then finally settling down to go to sleep.

It took me a while to actually get to sleep, there on the hard floor. The floor was carpeted, but, well, it was still a floor, and I was used to my comfy bed. After about an hour of not being able to fall asleep, I got up to use the bathroom, then came back and tried to arrange my blankets into a better position.

That was when I heard a whisper: "Alanna?"

I turned to see who was whispering to me. Madalaine was the closest one to me. Her eyes were open and
she was facing me.

"Yeah?" I whispered back.

"I think Shelly and Amanda are sleeping."

"Was I being too loud?" I asked guiltily.

"No, no, you're fine. I just... wanted to ask you
something."

"Okay." I settled back down into my sleeping bag
and propped myself up on my elbow, facing Madalaine.
She did the same thing.

"The boy who you almost kissed... it wasn't Daniel,
right?"

What? "No!" I exclaimed, forgetting to be quiet. I
lowered my voice and spoke in a whisper. "No, of course
not. Daniel likes *you.* It was his brother. Travis."

"Oh." Even in the dim light, I could see the relief
flowing over Madalaine's face. "Okay. I didn't really
think it would be Daniel, but... you said it was your
friend in your neighborhood... he's the one you play basketball with, right?"

I nodded.

"Oh. That's good." Madalaine hesitated, and I knew
she wanted to say more. "So... you don't like Daniel at

all, right? I mean, romantically? I know he's your best friend."

I know he's your best friend. Up until the beginning of seventh grade, I would have agreed with that. *Of course* Daniel was my best friend. But now… Daniel was still my friend, I knew that. But could I really call him my *best* friend?

I wasn't sure about that. I didn't know what to call Daniel anymore. But I knew one thing.

"I don't like him romantically," I said definitively. "I kind of… I kind of used to think I did. Even back at the beginning of the school year. I used to be jealous, like, when you guys were together and stuff, and when you first started dating. But that was more because Daniel and I used to be each other's only friends, basically, and he was starting to make more friends." In the dim light, I could see Madalaine start to look like she wanted to say something, but I just kept blabbering out my thoughts. "I always thought Daniel and I should be together. Because when we were little, we made all these plans about how we were going to grow up and get married and do everything together. I never really considered our lives turning out different from that. So I tried to make myself think I liked him as, like, a boyfriend, but really I only liked him as a friend."

"Are you *sure* you only like him as a friend?" asked Madalaine. "Because, I really like him, but you know that pact we made at the beginning of the year? I don't want to break that. And I'd feel really bad going out with Daniel if I knew you wanted to go out with him, 'cause you and him have been best friends since forever…"

"Madalaine," I said, looking right into her eyes. "Don't feel bad about going out with Daniel. I like you guys as a couple. And I really, truly don't like Daniel that way. I like Travis."

There. It was out, and it was how I really felt. *I like Travis.*

But now what was I supposed to do with that information?

Chapter 27

I Got This

We all stayed at Amanda's house until mid-afternoon the next day. We made giant waffles for breakfast, then spied on her family, played some more games, played soccer in the backyard with her brothers, and made jewelry with beads. We all wanted to stay the whole day and sleep over that night too, but all the parents said no.

I felt fine the whole time I was at Amanda's. Then Mom came and picked me up, and I started to feel nervous.

What in the world was I going to do about the whole Travis situation?

I decided to talk to Lacey when I got home. Lacey would be able to give me advice. And she'd known all along that I was the girl Travis liked.

I found Lacey in her room on her computer (surprise, surprise). "Hey," I said quietly.

Lacey didn't hear me. I noticed she had earbuds in. "Hey," I said, a little more loudly. I walked over and tapped Lacey's shoulder.

"Oh! You're back!" Lacey took one of her earbuds out and turned to face me better. "How was the sleepover?"

"Good."

"Was it kind of like the ones we used to have with Travis and Daniel?"

I nodded. "Kind of."

"Cool." Lacey put her earbud back in and started to turn back around.

"Wait! Lacey!"

Lacey paused, mid-turn.

"I need to talk to you about something important."

I almost expected Lacey to blow me off, say that nothing was more important than homework or something to that effect, but she didn't. Instead, she took both of her earbuds out and shut her laptop screen.

Then she turned all the way around to face me.

I now had my sister's full attention, but I couldn't think of anything to say.

"Does this have anything to do with how weird Travis has been acting lately?" Lacey asked.

This was news to me. "Travis has been acting weird? How?"

Lacey shrugged. "You know, moping around, not telling me much of anything. Not playing basketball with you every day."

I sighed and stared out the window. Lacey's window faced the Malones' house. I could see the basketball net and the driveway.

I finally got up the courage to ask Lacey the question. "Who's the girl Travis likes?"

Lacey didn't answer. I looked at her. "Who's the girl Travis likes?" I repeated.

"I'm not really supposed to tell you that," said Lacey.

I took a huge breath and asked, "Is it me?"

Lacey hesitated. I could tell she was torn between loyalty to her best friend and loyalty to her sister. I didn't want her to have to make that choice.

"That's okay, I know it's me," I said. I told her

about what had happened on Tuesday. Lacey seemed to be trying not to smile. "I have no idea what to do," I finished. "How do you do that, anyway? Let a boy know you like him?"

"I find it funny that you, of all people, are asking me, of all people, this question," said Lacey. "I haven't had a crush on anyone since third grade. I don't know much of anything about relationships and all that stuff. And you've always been so blunt and straightforward… I'm surprised you're asking what to do about a situation, rather than just doing something."

I couldn't tell if she was insulting me or not. "But… Travis is your best friend," I said, before realizing that that might not be the truth anymore. "Or at least your friend. And he told you that he liked me, so… wait. Why didn't he want me to know?"

Lacey looked at me incredulously. *"Why didn't he want you to know?* Think about it, Alanna. He's liked you since at least the end of the summer. But you were busy getting adjusted to junior high, and then you were all about Daniel, and you told me that you liked Daniel, so I told him that you liked Daniel, so… he didn't want to ruin anything by letting you know."

That made sense. Even now, when I really did like

Travis (and knew that I liked him), the almost-kiss had made things awkward between us.

"So… how do I fix it?" I asked.

Lacey shrugged. "Go talk to him, I guess."

"And tell him… what?"

Lacey looked at me straight on. "Be Alanna. Don't worry about what's the right thing to say or whether it'll sound weird or anything. Just speak from your heart."

It was some of the best advice she'd ever given me.

I got up and started heading out of the room. On the way out, I stopped and turned around. "Thanks, Lacey," I said.

She smiled and gave me a thumbs-up. "You can do it."

I didn't want to show it, but I was nervous as I walked across the grass connecting the two yards. How was Travis going to react when he saw me?

I went up the familiar front steps and rang the bell. *Please let this work out,* I prayed, squeezing my eyes shut and crossing my fingers.

I heard the door being opened, and I opened my eyes. "Hi Alanna," It was Daniel.

"Hi," I said. "Um, is Travis here?"

Daniel nodded. "You want to come in?"

"Sure."

I followed Daniel into the house, struck by a weird sense of déjà vu. Wasn't it just recently that I'd done this exact same thing, but the other way around? Up until just a couple weeks ago, hadn't I always asked for Daniel whenever Travis came to the door?

"I have no idea where he is, but he's in here somewhere," said Daniel, grinning apologetically. He had the same grin as Travis, but his grin didn't make me feel the way Travis's did. I could recognize that now.

"Travis!" called Daniel. "Alanna's here!"

Moments later, Travis came into the room, and I felt my heart start to beat a little faster. "Alanna," he said, stopping a few feet away from me. "Alanna... I'm really sorry."

"Why are you sorry?"

"For—" He glanced at Daniel. "For what happened last Tuesday."

I looked at Daniel too. He looked somewhat perplexed. I hoped what I was about to say next wouldn't hurt his feelings.

"I always used to think Daniel and I should be boyfriend and girlfriend," I said to Travis. "Because of what we planned when we were little. How I would marry Daniel, and you would marry Lacey, and we'd all live together in our next-door mansions. But I guess it's kind of silly to make all your life choices based on something you decided in kindergarten. Because people change their minds. And I've changed my mind."

I looked at Daniel, who didn't look upset at all, and then at Travis, who looked slightly hopeful, and at the same time slightly disbelieving. "I like Daniel as a friend," I said, smiling at Daniel, who smiled back. "And even though we both kind of have our own set of friends now, I hope we stay friends with each other too." Then I looked back toward Travis. "I like you as a friend too, but I also like you as a…" I couldn't think of the right word. *Boyfriend?* He wasn't technically my boyfriend, not yet anyway. *Crush?* Was that the word? Would that sound too weird?

Rather than saying anything, I went over to him and put my arms around his neck. I'd never done this before, and I wasn't really sure how I was supposed to do it, but I just started standing up on my tippy toes and moving my face toward his. And then I felt him put his arms around me, and he tilted his face down toward mine, and our lips touched each other.

My first kiss.

Travis and I broke apart and grinned at each other. We probably would have stood there grinning at each other for longer, except Daniel burst out, "That was the weirdest, most disgusting thing I've ever seen! I can't believe I just saw my best friend and my brother kiss each other! You guys are messed!"

"Well, I've had my first kiss now," I told him. "So now it's your turn. Next time you see Madalaine."

Daniel got that grin on his face—the one he always had when he was with Madalaine or when her name was mentioned—and I could tell he wasn't really mad or super grossed out or anything by Travis and me kissing each other. It was just weird for him to see it for the first time. He would get used to it.

"Hey," I said. "You guys wanna go out front and play some basketball?"

"Definitely," said Travis.

"Probably not," said Daniel. "You guys know I'm not that good."

"What better way to get better than to practice?" I asked. I took him by one arm and Travis took him by the other and we hauled him outside.

"Oh, *fine*," said Daniel, heaving a huge fake sigh. "I

guess since I'm already *out here*, I'll play."

"We could see if Lacey wants to join us," I suggested. "We could play two on two."

"I'll text her," said Travis.

Two minutes later, Lacey was jogging over, dressed in khakis and a sweater. "Wow," Travis commented, looking from her to Daniel. "You two have a lot to learn about basketball. But don't worry." He winked at me. "Alanna and I can teach you."

He passed the ball to me and I charged the net, tossing it up for a perfect layup.

Epilogue

We sat there under the oak tree between the two yards, all four of us. It was surprisingly warm for the second week in November, and for the first time in a while, all our schedules worked out and we were able to spend a Saturday together. Just like old times.

"Man," said Travis, leaning back into the grass. "What a nice day."

I smiled, because he'd done the exact same thing the last time we'd all been here, the day before I started junior high. So much had changed since then. But they were good changes, mostly. I would miss hanging out with Daniel and Travis and Lacey every single day, the way we used to when we were little. But I was happy with the way things were turning out.

"I'm glad we can still do this," Lacey commented. "You know, get together once in a while. I feel like I don't see you guys that much anymore. I mean, I see Alanna, obviously, and I see Travis at school, but we haven't hung out like this in a while. I haven't seen Daniel since, what, Halloween?"

"Nope, before that," said Daniel. "I wasn't here on Halloween, remember? I was at Max's party."

"Oh, that's right," said Lacey. "That's why it was just Travis and Alanna who went trick-or-treating. I was finishing up my paper, and you were at that party."

It had been weird, not having Daniel and Lacey with us when Travis and I went trick-or-treating, because every year since Daniel and I were babies, the four of us had always gone together. But it had been fun, all the same.

"I think the last time you saw me was the night of the dance," Daniel told Lacey. "When I came over to get a ride with Alanna."

"Right!" exclaimed Lacey. "And that was, what, three days before Halloween?"

"Yeah."

I smiled, remembering the dance. I'd ended up having a really good time. I'd wanted to bring Travis as my partner, but there was a rule that the only people allowed at the dance were people who actually went to our school, so I'd just gone by myself. Which had turned out okay, because actually, most people had just gone by themselves, so I didn't feel awkward or anything. And most of the dances had been big group dances anyway, and to be honest, we hadn't really even danced all that much. I'd hung out with Shelly and Amanda and Madalaine, and sometimes we were joined by Daniel and Hunter and Max and some of the other lunch table people. My friends had teased me about having a boyfriend who was in high school, and Shelly had said that if I was ever allowed to go to a high school dance with Travis, I'd probably come back thinking our junior high dance was really, really lame. But I'd disagreed. "It can't be lame if I'm hanging out with some of my best friends," I'd told her. "And I am!"

It was nice having more friends than just Daniel, Travis, and Lacey. I was becoming really close with Madalaine, Amanda, and Shelly, and already we were planning another sleepover for the four of us. And, to my great surprise, even Madalaine and Daniel's lunch table was starting to accept me as part of their group now that I was no longer trying to be Daniel's shadow.

But just because I had new friends, didn't mean I no longer wanted to spend time with my old ones.

"Guys," I said, looking around at my sister, my good friend, and my good friend/boyfriend. "We should keep doing this every so often. Hanging out together. I don't mean all the time, 'cause I know we all have our own stuff to do. But just like, maybe every month or so. Pick a day and all do something together."

"I'm down for that," said Travis.

"Me too," agreed Daniel.

"Yeah, that sounds good," said Lacey.

Daniel leaned back in the grass, matching Travis's pose, staring up at the sky. "D'you guys think we'll always be friends? Like even when we're all grown up?"

"I think we will as long as we make an effort to be," said Travis.

We were all silent for a little bit. Then Daniel spoke up again. "It's weird thinking about the future. Like where we'll all be in ten or twenty years. Or even five years."

"Harvard," said Lacey. "Or maybe Stanford. I haven't decided yet. I want to be a lawyer and live in New York City."

"I want to be a programmer," said Daniel. "Maybe

program video games or something. Or just computers. I don't really care where I live as long as I'm close to my job."

"I don't really know what I want to do yet," said Travis. "Probably something to do with sports, although not actually playing the sports for a living. I might want to be a coach, or maybe work with sports medicine. It'd be cool to work with some big team."

Everyone was looking at me now, waiting for me to tell them where I'd be in five or ten or twenty years, or what I wanted to do with my life. But the thing was, I wasn't really sure. I could see a lot of possible futures playing out before me. Maybe I'd become a professional basketball player. Maybe I'd be a coach or sports doctor, like Travis. Maybe I'd become an artist, or a YouTuber, or a chef, or something else. Maybe I'd marry Travis. I liked that possibility, me being a basketball player and him being a coach, and us being married, and having four kids and a couple dogs. But that was just in my imagination. I had no way of knowing whether any of that would actually come true. And you know what? I liked it that way. I didn't need to have every aspect of my life already planned out, because things could change at any time. I could change. My perspective could change. My hopes and dreams could change.

"I don't know where I'll be in five or ten years," I told Lacey, Travis, and Daniel. "I haven't really decided what I want to be when I grow up. But you know what? I'm okay with not knowing anything about the future. I'm okay with not having everything planned out yet. I'm good with just being a seventh-grader. Just enjoying the now."

"Enjoying the now," said Lacey. "I like that. No need to rush the future, I guess."

The conversation trailed off, and we all just sat there for a moment, enjoying our time together. Then the breeze picked up, and I saw Daniel shiver slightly in his T-shirt and shorts. "I'm getting cold just sitting here. You guys want to go ride bikes or something?" he asked.

"Sounds good to me," said Travis. Lacey and I nodded.

We all got up and went to get our bikes, then reconvened out on the road.

"Which way do we want to go?" asked Travis.

I looked up and down the street. One way, past our house, we'd stay in our neighborhood and get primarily flat ground. Nice and predictable. The other way, past the Malones' house, we'd end up on the next street over, with the big, steep hill. We'd have to go up it before we could go down, but once we reached the top, we'd get to cruise down it at full speed. After that would come a series of smaller hills, going up and down and up and down. It was more work, but it was also more fun.

"Let's go this way." I started pedaling in the direction past the Malones' house. Travis, Lacey, and Daniel followed.

The future was an open road, stretching out ahead of me. Maybe it would be easy. Maybe it wouldn't. I didn't know where any of us would be one year from now, let alone five or ten. But I wasn't going to worry about or try to control the future.

It was time to enjoy the now.

A Note From The Author

I started my first full-time job in fall 2015, working as a middle school paraprofessional. On certain days of the week, I had a little bit of free time at the beginning or end of the school day. I decided it would be fun to try to write an entire book over the course of the school year, only working on the book while I was at school.

At first, writing Alanna's story was just something to do. As the year went on, though, I found myself getting more and more interested in it. When January rolled around, I started arriving at school 20 minutes earlier than I used to—because the earlier I arrived, the more time I had to write!

No matter how excited I was about adding to the story, I only allowed myself to work on it at school. Every time I opened the document, I would read the last couple lines of what I'd written, and then continue from there. I didn't edit. I didn't read back on previous chapters. Sometimes I wrote for twenty minutes at a time, sometimes I wrote for two. Sometimes I knew exactly what was going to happen, other times I made things up on the spot.

I took a long-term sub position (at the same middle school) in April, and that threw me off from my writing a little at first. I suddenly had so much more to do for my job! But I got into the swing of it eventually, and by the end of May I truly believed that I would have the book done by the last day of school.

I remember the morning of the second-to-last day of school, when I finally finished the last chapter and only had the epilogue left to write. I was so excited! That day, I stayed in my hot classroom until nearly 6pm, finishing the last of my school-related tasks, and then, finally, writing the epilogue to my Alanna story. I still remember the feeling that went through me when I finally typed out the last line. The feeling of, "Whoa… I'm *done*. I actually finished the book! Before the end of the school year!!!!!!"

I printed it out immediately, and started reading as soon as I got home. Due to the way I'd written it (tiny piece by tiny piece with no editing), I didn't expect it to be very good. I was pleasantly surprised. It needed a few tweaks here and there, but overall it was a solid book!

Whenever I read *I Didn't Plan This*, I see two stories simultaneously playing out in my head. First and foremost, I see the story of Alanna, Travis, Daniel, Lacey, Madalaine, and the rest of the characters. Behind all that, however, I see the classrooms I was in as I wrote and mentally plotted, and the students I interacted with throughout it all. Being in a middle school as I was writing a middle school book was quite helpful—it lent a lot of authenticity to the way the characters acted, thought, and talked. None of the characters are based off of any specific kids I knew, even those whose names happen to overlap (since I was always trying to write as much as I could in a short amount of time, I just gave new characters the first names that popped into my head) However, many of the interactions among various characters are pulled from the collective interactions I witnessed over the year.

Special thanks to all my students from Elm Street Middle School, 2015-2016: Aidan T, Allison G, Ally A, Amanda D, Angelica M, Anthony S, Antonio R, Ashley D, Ashton G, Ayden B, Ben C, Brady S, Brayden L, Bryan G, Caleb M, Chris M, Christian L, Cody S, Cooper A, Corey O, Corina M, Daija D, Daniela R, Davante D, Deven A, Devyn L, Diana A, Dominick M, Donovan L, Dustin V, Elijah C, Erien C, Frailin D, Frank B, Gabrielle P, Genesis M, Grace B, Guat T, Hailey N, Haley M, Hamza G, Hunter M, Ivan S, Jacob B, Jahmicah W, Jaiven S, Jason B, Jason P, Jazlyn G, Jeffrey P, Joshua B, Josiah J, Julious C, Justin M, Laci D, Leonardo M, Lila B, Luis N, Mabel W, Malia M, Megan W, Micah H, Michael Q, Nala C, Nate C, Nevan S, Nick E, Noah A, Owen G, Patrick O, Richard W, River F, Robert C, Samantha D, Seth B, Tim Z, TJ K, Travis G, Trey P, and Wol T. Also to Emily C, Emily D, Gabe A, Hailey M, Hayden B, Imoni S, Jocelyn S, Kelsey L, Kemenah W, Kyle T, Marc L, Sahiris F, Troy R, and Tianna P, who were never officially "my" students but still kept things fun and interesting!

All 95 of you made this book possible without even realizing it. Some of you I worked with as a para, others I had in my classes once I took on the teaching position. Some of you I got to know very well, others I didn't. Some of you will remember me, others won't. All of you are valuable, unique, and loved, and I wish you the best in the future.

About The Author

Kelsey Gallant was born in Bloomington, Indiana, in 1993. When she was little, she enjoyed dictating books to her mom and telling stories to her younger brother. Now she is the author of the Allisen's Notebooks series, *New Life*, and the short story *Out of My League*.

Ironically, Kelsey was homeschooled and therefore never actually attended junior high. However, she spent three years working as a middle school paraprofessional, and currently teaches math to 7th and 8th graders in Nashua, New Hampshire. When not writing or working, Kelsey enjoys reading, singing, being outside, and spending time with her family and friends.

Other Books by Kelsey Gallant

Allisen's Notebooks Series:
6ᵗʰ Grade With My Crazy Classmates, My Super Smart Sister, & Me
7ᵗʰ Grade With My Fabulous Friends, My New Neighbors, & Me
8ᵗʰ Grade With My Awesome Adventures, My Various Visitors, & Me
9ᵗʰ Grade With My Expanding Experiences, My Roller-coaster Relationships, & Me
10ᵗʰ Grade With My Interesting Interactions, My Terrific Travels, & Me

Allisen's Notebooks Super Special E-Shorts:
Mirisen
Jack
Shevea
Kim
Harrisson
Stivre
America the Beautiful

New Life series:
New Life

Stand-Alone Short Stories:
Auf Wiedersehen, Привет
Out of My League

Made in the USA
Las Vegas, NV
16 November 2023

80974198R00146